GENESIS

BONES TRILOGY

PAIGE P. HORNE

Copyright ©2020 Paige P. Horne. All rights reserved.

This book is a work of fiction. Names, characters, place, events and other elements portrayed herein are either the product of the author's imagination or used fictitiously. Any resemblance to real persons or events is coincidental.

No part of this book may be reproduced or transmitted in any form or by any means, electronic or mechanical, including photography, recording, or an information storage and retrieval system without the prior consent from the publisher and author, except in the instance or quotes for reviews.

No part of this book may be uploaded without the permission of the publisher and author, nor be otherwise circulated in any form of binding or cover other than that in which it is originally published.

Paige P. Horne

Also, by Paige P. Horne	*5*
Chapter One	*9*
Chapter Two	*13*
Chapter Three	*23*
Chapter Four	*25*
Chapter Five	*32*
Chapter Six	*33*
Chapter Seven	*50*
Chapter Eight	*56*
Chapter Nine	*70*
Chapter Ten	*75*
Chapter Eleven	*86*
Chapter Twelve	*89*
Chapter Thirteen	*104*
Chapter Fourteen	*105*
Chapter Fifteen	*118*
Chapter Sixteen	*120*
Chapter Seventeen	*136*
Chapter Eighteen	*141*
Chapter Nineteen	*151*
Chapter Twenty	*153*
Chapter Twenty-One	*167*
Chapter Twenty-Two	*172*

Genesis

Chapter Twenty-Three	*177*
Chapter Twenty-Four	*178*
Chapter Twenty-Five	*194*
Chapter Twenty-Six	*197*
Chapter Twenty-Seven	*206*
Chapter Twenty-Eight	*208*
Chapter Twenty-Nine	*223*
Chapter Thirty	*240*
Chapter Thirty-One	*248*
Chapter Thirty-Two	*255*
Chapter Thirty-Three	*257*
Chapter Thirty-Four	*268*
Chapter Thirty-Five	*270*
Chapter Thirty-Six	*279*

Paige P. Horne

Also, by Paige P. Horne

A standalone
Close To Falling

The Chasing Series
Chasing Fireflies
Chasing Ellie

A standalone
If I'd Known

The Give Me Series
Start the series for **Free!**
Give Me Love
Give Me Perfect Love
Give Me Forever Love
Give Me Redemption

Cover designer: Cover It Designs
Editor: Paige Maroney Smith
Proofreader: Julie T

Genesis

Dedication: To all the little black hearts. This one's for you.

2020 Crime (Projected Data) for Postings, New Jersey (Southside)

Aggravated Assault	1,286
Arson	15
Burglary	1,041
Larceny and Theft	1,634
Motor Vehicle Theft	50
Murder and Manslaughter	86
Rape	90
Robbery	738
Crime Rate (Total Incidents)	4,580
Property Crime	2,697
Violent Crime	2,277

Genesis

For there is not a just man upon earth, that doeth good, and sinneth not.

~Ecclesiastes 7:20 KJV

Ye are of your father the devil, and the lusts of your father ye will do. He was a murderer from the beginning, and abode not in the truth, because there is no truth in him. When he speaketh a lie, he speaketh of his own: for he is a liar, and the father of it.

~John 8:44 KJV

For all have sinned, and come short of the glory of God.

~Romans 3:23 KJV

Chapter One

Bones
First day missing

Fear.
Fear is said to be an unpleasant emotion caused by the belief that someone or something is dangerous, likely to cause pain, or a threat.

My mind is a hazy prison cell with melting walls and a twirling floor. I feel my head fall to the side as my eyes blink open to darkness. My brain pounds against an achy skull as I catch the faint drip of water in the distance.

"You're up." I hear.

"Who's there?" I ask, hardly recognizing my own voice. I cough to remove the dryness in my throat.

Where the fuck am I?

My heart hammers against ribs I realize are bruised when I shift in the uncomfortable chair. My hands move, and I gasp when plastic digs into my skin around my wrists and my biceps. The feel of cotton against my face confirms I have on a blindfold.

"Don't worry about that," he says, his tone unfamiliar. He's using a voice disguiser.

Genesis

"Knowledge is a gift. I think you told me that one time."

"I told you that, huh? So, I know you then?" I try to clear my foggy mind, wishing this headache would stop. I laugh lightly, shaking my head. "Do you know what you've done?" I say acidly.

"I'm very aware of what I've done, Bones."

"As long as you're aware then." I wiggle my hands, feeling the zip tie cut into my flesh. I try to recall how I got here, but the drugs in my system keep my memory blocked. "What do you want?"

He laughs. "I want what you got to have."

I scoff, tasting copper when I lick my bottom lip. "And what's that?"

"Satisfaction."

This time I laugh. "Well, you got the wrong person, my man. I haven't had satisfaction in years."

I hear a groan coming from the other side of the room, and my throat closes.

Bexley. She was with me. We were attacked going to the flower shop where she works.

Anger and that fear I mentioned earlier consume my veins, forcing the fog completely from my mind. Dread fills the room. It's so real, I can feel its skin as it wraps its hands around my throat, constricting the air that begs to enter.

"Bexley, you all right?" I ask, tilting my head to the side so I can hear her again. Goddammit, I can't see shit. I don't know if she's hurt. I move, making the chair screech across the floor.

"She's fine," the stranger says. "She won't always be, but for now, she's fine."

"What the fuck does that mean?" I wiggle more, noticing my legs are also zip tied to the bottom of the chair.

"It means exactly what I said. You're not getting this, man. I plan to take everything from you. Including her."

I turn my head, spotting a light through a sheer spot in the cotton over my eyes. It pours in from somewhere, but it's natural, not from the glow of a bulb.

"You will know the pain I've felt."

I slightly flinch at his sudden closeness. I breathe in, trying to see if I recognize his scent.

"I will remove the people you care about one by one, and you, Danny O'Brien, won't be able to do anything about it."

What? The pain he's felt? What the hell is this?

"Look, motherfucker, you don't want to do this."

I feel his presence move away from me and hear the crunch of dirt beneath his shoes before a door squeaks open.

"Hey," I call out, moving my hands and shoulders widely. "You piece of shit," I seethe, moving frantically. The chair tips and I hit the hard

Genesis

floor, my head bouncing off the wooden floor, and then blackness consumes my mind.

Chapter Two
Danny
1998

We stare at Johnny's house from across the road. It's quiet and one street over from where I sleep. My heart drums to a steady beat. My palms are clammy, and my knees are shaky from what we are about to do. We've talked about this, late at night when everyone else was dreaming. Johnny has told me how he's had thoughts about getting rid of his old man. We've fantasized about how we'd do it.

    I look to Johnny for some sign of hesitation, but his focus is on the house he lives in. His jaw is locked, his eyes tight. I look back at the house. The sheer curtain cancels privacy, revealing a lamp sitting on a table near the window.

    The screen door is wide open, the wind lightly tapping it against the side of the wooden house. The front steps are bent and the paint peels in curls. The houses are different on this street. They're broken down, like the people inside of them.

    The moon is bright, and the clouds are a wisp of dark aluminum, setting a portentous backdrop. The tree's leaves in the backyard rustle when a summer

Genesis

breeze blows in, making the air taste like heat and choices that may save my friend and put us both away. We share a smoke I ganked from Ma after Johnny went back in and put his clothes on. It's not the first time I've smoked, but I feel light-headed and I'm not sure it's from the cigarette or the anxiousness swarming in my belly. I offer it to him, but he shakes his head.

"Let's roll," he says.

I nod and toss the smoke, hearing it sizzle from a puddle of rainwater left over from the thunderstorm that just came through. We look around, making sure no one sees us before we dart across the road, cutting our way across the freshly cut lawn, before we make it to the chain-link fence.

Johnny pulls the latch and we pass through the small gate. The backyard is made up of dirt and gravel with some pieces of grass sticking up. The old shed has seen better days, and the lean-to looks to be one good burst of wind from falling.

I spot the shelf of moonshine Johnny mentioned earlier. "It'll make sense for my fingerprints to be on everything," he says to me. "But not yours." He walks past the shelf and grabs something from a makeshift table. "Here."

I take the tan oil-stained gloves. "I don't think we have to worry about fingerprints, Johnny."

Paige P. Horne

"Dude, we've watched enough crime shows. You can never be too careful. I don't want to end up in juvie facing a prison sentence. Do you?"

I search his eyes, something clicking inside of me. I've done a lot of little crimes—stolen things and smashed car windows playing stickball in the street. I've broken into the school and vandalized some old buildings, but I've never done anything like this.

This is murder.

This is premeditated, straight-up first degree. To the world we're kids. But right now, we're two men deciding to take another's life because…well…. he deserves it.

"Never get caught," I say.

He nods. "Never get caught."

We exchange a look right then, one that bonds us together for life. Johnny is my brother, not by blood, but where it counts. We chose each other, and brothers have each other's backs no matter what.

I'm doing this for Johnny.

I slide the gloves on, and we each take a handful of jars and head back toward the house. The moon is hidden now, so I follow Johnny as we creep up the back porch steps. He adjusts the jars in his hands and turns the knob before we pass through

Genesis

the doorway. I turn and click the door back shut quietly before twisting around. I've never been in his house before. He's always come to mine. I do a quick scan of dirty dishes piled in the kitchen sink. Roaches scatter at my feet, and the cabinet doors are open below the sink. Tools sit in front of it, as a continuous drip falls from the faucet above. I guess Johnny's dad thought about fixing the leak.

Johnny doesn't seem embarrassed by his house. In fact, he seems more confident than I've ever seen him. His back is straight, his shoulders squared. My best friend's chin is lifted as he white-knuckles the jar in his clenched fist. His hair is buzzed short and the scar on his head I've always noticed but never asked about glows silver in the darkness.

We exit the kitchen, heading down a long hallway. There's a bathroom to the left and I hear the sound of snoring coming up ahead.

Anxiousness fills me. I swallow as we enter the living room. Johnny's dad is passed out in a dirty orange cloth chair. There's a jar at his feet, its contents consumed. Worn boots sit by a tattered couch and a stack of newspapers rests by a crate used as a table that has *fragile* written and fading away on it. A pack of Camels and a weathered Zippo lighter sit on top of it, along with an ashtray and some junk mail.

Paige P. Horne

I see a photo of a woman, Johnny's dad, and Johnny from years ago hanging crooked on the wall. That must have been his mom. I don't ask him, though; he never talks about her. Part of me wonders if his old man beat her, too. Maybe he killed her?

"Start pouring," Johnny whispers.

"Don't get it on you," I say, twisting the cap off. The place fills with overpowering fumes as we both begin drenching everything in moonshine, soaking the couch and all the furniture.

Johnny stops and looks at his old man, studying him as though he wants this moment captured in his memory for the rest of his life. I've seen him a few times, sitting on the porch when we'd come by on our bikes, never up close, though. Johnny looks like him, but not in an obvious way. Just the same face structure and hair color.

"Do you think he'll wake up?" I ask, slightly out of breath.

"I hope so," Johnny says.

And then he pours juice onto his dad's lap. The bastard still doesn't move. Johnny reaches down and grabs the man's smokes. Pulling one out, he scoops up the Zippo. He flicks it open, looking over it for a moment.

Genesis

"He's always had this," he says. "I can't tell you how many times I've had to buy lighter fluid for it." He studies the lighter in his hand, tracing the scratches and running his thumb over the brass. "He told me his father had it before him. Of all the things you can pass down to someone, my grandpa gave my old man a lighter." He looks over at me.

"Guess he didn't have anything else to give," I say.

He scoffs. "Guess not."

My boy lights the cigarette, takes one big drag, and thumps it onto the couch.

Flames shoot up from the drenched threading and quickly begin to spread, filling the room with toxic smoke.

"Shit," I say, putting my shirt over my nose. "Come on."

Johnny grabs the family photo off the wall, leaving a clean spot behind and revealing how much these walls are nicotine-stained. I toss the moonshine, hearing it shatter as we take off through the hall. Johnny leaves a trail of homebrew behind us, drenching the countertops in the kitchen. He tosses the Mason jar and we hurry from the house, running through the yard and across the street. We dip into the alleyway, and Johnny stops and turns around.

Paige P. Horne

"We shouldn't be here," I say to him.

"Just give me a second," he says. We both stand watching the house as the fire consumes it. Smoke pours from the cracks, red flames bellow behind the windows, and then the glass breaks.

"You didn't want anything else in there?" I ask, looking down at the photo in his hand.

Johnny shakes his head, opening his hand. "Nah, I got my family heirloom."

I look at the Zippo and smirk. "Yeah, I guess you do."

"Think he's dead yet?" he asks.

"I don't know. I feel like he would have woken up yelling if he wasn't." I cross my arms over my chest. "I think I read somewhere that it only takes a few minutes to die from smoke inhalation."

"Kinda wish he would have woken up. Suffered a little, ya know?" Johnny says in a serious tone.

I lift a brow. This boy's dad is burning alive in that house because of us and he wishes he would have suffered a little more? That's messed up, but I guess if you've been beaten as many times as he has, it's understandable.

"Hey, he had a Viking funeral," I say with a smirk.

"Minus the boat," Johnny says. "And the fact he wasn't dead first."

Genesis

We both twist back when we hear something behind a dumpster. "Hey," I call out.

My eyes grow wide when a girl walks out from behind the bin. Wearing blue jean shorts and hot pink socks with black boots, she looks from me to Johnny before skipping her eyes past us at the burning house.

"Shit," Johnny says under his breath as sirens ring in the distance.

"We gotta bounce," I say evenly, looking at the stranger. I narrow my eyes at her before we take off running back home.

Out of breath, we all stop once we near my house. Johnny looks over at her. "Who the hell are you?" he says.

"Did you guys really set that house on fire?" she asks, sliding a piece of dark hair behind her ear.

I stand up straighter. "What's it to you if we did?"

I see her swallow in the moonlight, but there's a sense of curiosity in her expression. And then she shocks me. Her shoulders lift in a shrug. "I guess you got your reasons."

"Swear to us that you won't say anything," Johnny says.

She rolls her eyes. "I swear." She bites her inner cheek. "Was there someone in there?"

I dart my eyes to Johnny. The streetlamp shines above us, painting us in dim yellow, allowing me to see his face and hers.

"What happened to your face?" she asks him.

His tongue darts out and he licks the cut his father gave him only hours before.

"Don't worry about it," he says. "Who are you?"

She's quiet for a moment, studying Johnny and me. "I'm Bexley Walker. Just moved there," she says, pointing to the house right beside ours. I see the moving truck in the driveway.

"Well, Bexley Walker, you better keep your mouth shut about what you saw," I say to her.

"I wouldn't tell," she says.

"If you know what's good for you, you'll keep your word. I'm going inside," Johnny says, holding on to the arm his dad bruised earlier today. He walks away from us, heading toward the house.

I exhale, hearing the commotion of a fire truck and men yelling a street over.

"I'm not going to say anything," Bexley says again.

Genesis

"That's what you said," I reply. I walk off, because I don't care to stand here and talk to this girl. She was spying on us, and because of that, we now have someone who knows our secret. Someone who could get us caught.

"What's your name, anyway?" she asks.

"Danny," I say over my shoulder. "Keep your promise."

Chapter Three
Bexley
First day missing

"Danny," I say into the darkness. I wish I could see, make out where we are. My stomach growls in protest, and my head feels weightless. My shoulders ache from my arms being tied behind my back, and my wrists feel slit from rubbing against the plastic that cages them.

I woke up hours ago, but I've been fading in and out of consciousness, slipping in and out of memories.

Being unconscious is better, because I get a break from the reality of our situation. We're in an abandoned building, I think, although I can't see shit. Rats scurry across the floor, water leaks from somewhere, and Danny hasn't said a word since I thought I heard him call my name hours ago. My mouth is dry, my throat raw.

"Danny," I say again. "Wake up!"

Goddamn you. *Hate* is not a strong enough word for what I feel toward Danny O'Brien. I loathe him and everything he stands for. I close my eyes, wishing I were back with my husband. Wishing my life had turned out differently. Wishing I could beg my mama not to have moved us to the south side of

Genesis

Postings. Opening my eyes, I stare into the darkness, and without wanting to, I think back on a past that seems so long ago, and yet, I can still recall every last detail...

Chapter Four
Bexley
1998

I watch Danny's back as he walks to his house. The other kid is already inside, with a busted face and an arm that looked like it was hurt. I turn toward the flames blazing one street over. Smoke fills the night sky, turning black to gray. I wonder about those boys and why they set that house on fire.

Neither one of them seems like nice kids.

I start school Monday and I was hoping to make some friends in my new neighborhood, but it doesn't look like I'm going to do that. I hate this place already, except for the boy who just walked away from me.

He's the cutest thing I've ever seen, but who cares about that. I've got more important things to worry about. Like my mom in there.

My heart seizes up, the muscle tired of what it knows the future holds.

Mom thinks I'm stupid. I know why she moved us here. It's closer to her brother, the man who's probably going to raise me. I've cried so many nights alone in my bedroom. I've shed every last tear in my body, I honestly don't think I have any more left.

Genesis

Kicking a rock, I twist back and head toward my own house. The one right next to theirs. I hurry up the steps and open the door. My ears perk when I step into the living room. Mom is coughing again. I swipe the door shut behind me and hurry up the stairs to her room.

"Mom?" I say, pushing her cracked door open. She sits on her bed in her nightgown, looking down at a napkin in her hand.

My eyes go to it.

Crimson stains the white.

She quickly balls it up, but it's too late. She's coughing up blood now.

"Hey, baby," she says. "You okay?"

"Am I okay?" I ask. "You're coughing up blood, Mama."

She swallows, her brown eyes switching from trying to protect me to the truth. "Come here," she says, patting her bed. I walk over slowly, sitting on the end of her bed instead of right where she touched the comforter. There's something happening. Something I didn't even notice until it was already in full effect.

I'm pulling away from her. My body is trying to protect itself from pain.

The pain of losing her.

She looks down for a moment before lifting her chin. "You're old enough to know the truth," she says. "The cancer has spread."

Paige P. Horne

My chest rips open, and my heart bleeds and weeps. But my face stays emotionless. "How long?" I ask. I sound like I've aged ten years asking that question. I'm surely the oldest eleven-year-old on the planet. I pull on my snap bracelet.

She shrugs. "They don't know for sure." A tear rolls down her cheek, but her face doesn't crack. She always tries to be strong for me. I look down at the comforter, grabbing a loose string and twirling it around my finger.

"Well, I guess there's no use in unpacking my things then, is there? Tell me, why did you move us in this house? Why didn't we just move into Uncle Hale's?" I get off the bed. "That would make more sense, wouldn't it? Since you're going to die and leave me."

"Bexley," Mama says, sitting up and reaching out to me. But I shake my head and run out of the room. I take off down the stairs and yank the door open, running out into the street. The fire still roars in the night sky, just like the fire I feel inside of me.

Life's not fair.

I look to the left of me, balling my fists. I want to scream to the top of my lungs, but instead, I take off running down the road. I run as fast and hard as I can until I get to an alleyway near some abandoned buildings.

Out of breath, I lean my back against the wall and wipe the sweat from my brow. I shut my eyes

Genesis

for a moment as my mind runs. I'm not going to have a mom in my future. The one person I've always had is going to leave me.

My heart thumps sadly, distraught and feeble. How will I live? What will I do?

Opening my eyes, I look down and spot a rock. I pick it up and push off the wall. My eyes go to the windows above the building and I rare back and throw the rock as hard as I can, immensely satisfied when it shatters the glass. Shards sprinkle down like fallen rain, hitting the cement below my feet.

"You always take off running down dark streets?" I hear. I snap my head behind me.

A boy older than me, with dark hair and clothes too nice for this neighborhood, stands with his hands in his pockets.

"Did you follow me?"

Danny shrugs. "I was sitting on the roof and saw you take off. I was curious to see where a little girl like you could be going at this time of night."

"Why?" I ask.

"I'm a curious person."

"No, I mean, why were you sitting on the roof?"

He lifts a brow and his chin at the same time. "Thinking," he says.

"About?"

He studies me for a moment, and then he removes his hands from his pockets and reaches down to pick up a rock. He chunks it at one of the windows, and again the glass meets the ground.

"Why are you out here?" he asks, clearly not going to tell me what he was thinking about on the roof of his house. He must have gotten down pretty quickly to catch up to me. Or maybe I'm not as fast a runner as I think I am.

"I needed to get out of the house." I pick up another piece of granite and break a third window.

"Why is that?" he asks.

I shrug. "Arguing with my mom."

"About?"

"You sure are nosy," I say.

He smirks. "Curious."

I roll my eyes. "Curiosity killed the cat. Don't you know that?"

He laughs and my knees get weak, my stomach tightens, and I suddenly feel light-headed.

"I'm not going to die," he says.

"We all die," I reply.

He shakes his head and lifts another rock. "Not me. I'm going to live forever." He throws it toward the windows.

"That's impossible, dummy."

"Nothing's impossible," he says. "Don't you want to live forever?"

I shrug, knowing all too well what death looks like to believe anyone could outrun it.

He stops and looks at me peculiarly.

Genesis

I pick up a rock and throw it with everything inside of me. My mom's dying and I'm here throwing rocks at windows with some boy I don't even know.

"Hey!" someone yells. We both look back at the person with a flashlight.

"Shit," Danny says. "Come on." He grabs my hand and we take off running.

"Hey! Come back here," the man yells after us, but Danny makes us go lightning speed. I can hardly keep up. He grips my hand like a kid afraid to lose their balloon. We exit the alleyway and round the corner, heading back toward our houses.

My legs hurt from running so fast, and my arm burns from being pulled. Danny looks behind us as we slow down. He drops my hand, and that's when I realize that was the first time I've ever held a boy's hand.

He looks at me and smiles. "That's always so fun."

"What?" I ask, out of breath.

"Doing something bad and not getting caught," he replies like it's the simplest thing.

I make a face of confusion. "You like doing bad things?"

"Don't you?" he asks. "You were the one busting windows first."

"I was... I wasn't doing it because it was bad. I was doing it because I was mad."

"What's the difference in why? You still knew it was wrong and you still did it. And…" he says all matter-of-factly, "you didn't get caught."

My mouth opens to respond, but I realize he's right.

He exhales and then looks back at his house. "Don't go running off at night anymore. This neighborhood isn't safe. Especially for little girls."

"I'm not a little girl."

He smirks. "Yes, you are. See you around, Bexley Walker." He turns and heads to his house, and I stand in the street watching my first crush disappear.

Chapter Five

Bones
One day missing

My eyes move behind closed lids, but I don't wake. I dream.
Floating constantly and never getting a grip on consciousness. Somewhere in the distance, I can hear Bexley call my name, but she sounds odd. Her voice echoes through my mind, but I can't reach her. It's like I'm running in slow motion, never going fast enough and getting nowhere...

Chapter Six
Danny
1998

The piercing sting of smoke has disappeared from the horizon as sharp rays of sunlight slip through heaven-sent, crystal-clear water. It sprays with an angry force, shooting onto the sizzling pavement. The Jersey sun browns our skin, creating freckles and lines beneath that'll show when we grow older. Paul, the oldest of us three boys, tosses the skateboard at me.

"Go already," he says.

I flick him off, my eyes looking back at the water spewing from the fire hydrant at the bottom of the cement hill. We've only got one board and it's not even ours.

Well, it is now.

I ganked it from a stupid preppy at school while he was taking a piss in the outside bathroom. We're dirt poor, just like everyone else on this side of town. Our mom grew up in a Catholic home. Our dad was Irish. He was doing business here in the US when he and Mom fell in love. He moved her to Ireland, but things changed, and they moved to the States when Mom was pregnant with Paul, but Dad

Genesis

didn't let us forget that side of him. He made us learn our Irish background and be proud of the Irish blood running through our veins. He even took us back there a few times.

But Dad was into some bad shit, which resulted in a very bad ending for him and our mom. They died when I was nine. Grandparents on Mom's side were the only ones left to take us in, so that's where we ended up. Pa died last year of a heart attack, so it's just Ma raising three boys.

She's a saint.

We're not.

I spit onto the street before I place one foot on the grip tape. Popping the crick in my neck from falling asleep on the floor watching *The Sandlot* for the hundredth time, I ready myself.

"Tie your shoe, dumbass," Paul says. I lean down and do a quick loop, pulling tight before licking my finger and removing a scuff on my high-top Reebok. We may be poor, but my brothers and I do yard work in the richer neighborhoods, so we don't have to look it. Plus, we have sticky fingers and sometimes we take without asking.

"Are you going to go or what?" Paul says.

"Shut up," I throw back, looking over at our youngest brother, Samuel. He stands shirtless with his hands in his pockets. The sun shining on his head turns his brown hair copper. "You're next," I say.

"No way, Danny." He shakes his head. "You two are idiots."

"Don't be a pussy," I tell him. "You've got to grow some balls, man."

"His haven't dropped yet," Paul says with a snicker.

Samuel lifts his chin, looking confused and shy all at once. "What does that mean?"

I laugh and shake my head. "You'll figure it out." I look over at my best friend Johnny. He doesn't do yard work, so his clothes *are* shit, but we wear the same size, so I let him borrow mine sometimes when his are looking really rough. Today, though, we look alike—no shirt, cut-off jean shorts, and high-top Reeboks that we three bought for him.

"I'm next," he states.

I lift my lip.

That's my boy.

No one has even asked us any questions about Johnny's old man burning up in that house a few days ago. The fire department called it an accident. Said he probably passed out with a jar of moonshine and a lit cigarette. Everyone knew his dad was the town drunk and he loved his smokes.

Genesis

Fire and one hundred proof alcohol isn't a good combo—just saying. Everyone is relieved Johnny wasn't in the house asleep, too. It's a big deal in the neighborhood. All the moms have come by Ma's to check on Johnny and bring plates of food.

It's been a good couple of days, but unfortunately, that's all going to change. Ma says child services are going to come get Johnny. He'll be put in the system, but that doesn't matter. We've already talked about it. We'll figure out a way for him to come back here.

I kick off the pavement and place my other foot on the board, lifting my arms out for balance. The wind licks my sun-kissed skin and I grin because, holy shit, this is fun. Flying down the hill, I near the bottom at lightning speed, feeling the trickle of water rain down on my bare shoulders and back as I grow closer to the fire hydrant.

I shut my eyes for a moment, relishing in the feeling of flying, and then I slam into something hard and bony that knocks the oxygen from my lungs.

"Shit," I curse as I flip over the hard object and slide on my back, feeling the pavement rip me to shreds.

I struggle to take in air and wince at the burn coming from my torn flesh.

"How did you not see me?" a girl's voice says, sounding as if she's in agony, too.

I blink my eyes and look over at the girl in a flowery bathing suit getting up from the soaked ground.

Bexley.

She looks at her busted elbow and touches her bleeding jaw.

"How did *you* not see me?" I ask, turning and placing my palms down so I can stand up. Tiny pieces of gravel dig into my palms.

"Oh snap," Johnny says, running up. "You all right, man?"

"No," I reply, looking at Bexley as I wipe little rocks from my hands.

She's not crying like any other girl would, and it makes me even more curious about her.

"It's you again," he says.

"And it's you again," she throws back. I look past Johnny as my brothers come running up. They can't know we've already met; there will be too many questions.

"You don't know us," I say to her in warning. She doesn't respond, just blinks at me.

"What did I tell you about hitting girls?" Paul says as he and Samuel join us at the bottom of the hill. He whacks me on the head. I wince, swatting my arm at him. "I don't hit girls. She jumped in front of me."

"You all right?" he asks her, ignoring me.

"Totally," she says sarcastically.

Paul's fifteen and the oldest of all of us. He's also a con artist. He's making Bexley think he really cares because he doesn't want me to get into more trouble. I get into enough.

"Why don't you come to our house and I can fix you up? We have butterfly stiches. That'll probably do the trick. It's not that bad."

"As if," she says. "I'm not going with all you boys." She turns on her heel and heads to the house next to ours. The moving truck that was parked there a few days ago is gone. She's officially our new neighbor.

Paul shoves my shoulder. "How did you not see her?" he says.

"I closed my eyes for one second."

"You closed your eyes while you were flying down a hill on a skateboard?" he says.

"That's what I said."

He shakes his head. "You really do have a death wish, boy."

"She lives next door," Samuel says, looking after her like he's seen an angel or some shit.

I smirk. "Looks like Samuel's got a crush."

"Do not," he says, his face turning as red as the fire hydrant. I look toward the girl's house, something inside of me oddly wishing I could tell Samuel I met her first, but I shove that shit away as I look over my shoulder, trying to see my back. It's burning like crazy.

Paul spins me around. "Come on," he says. "We need to clean you up."

I reach down and scoop the board up before we four start to walk up to the house, forgetting about busted fire hydrants when we hear the sirens approaching. Someone must have reported the water.

Johnny pulls open the metal door, wincing when he does. His arm is still sore.

"You might need to get that checked out," Paul says.

"Nah, I'd know if it was broken," Johnny replies. Over a year ago, Johnny's dad snapped that same arm with a baseball bat. But that's not all that's happened. The boy's been choked, punched, and even had a rib fractured. He took it all like a champ, but it was sick and twisted.

I have zero regrets about what we did.

My brothers haven't suspected a thing, and so far, Bexley has kept her word.

Genesis

"I guess you'd know," Paul says. I drop the board in the foyer and we four kick our shoes off.

"Go wash up, boys," Ma yells from the kitchen.

I shove Samuel into the wall and take off running up the stairs with him right on my tail. At the top of the step, he grabs my foot and trips me. I bite my tongue when my cheek lands on the old hardwood, but turn around and yank his arm down before twisting him so his back is on my front. I wrap my legs around his waist and put him in a chokehold as he taps my arm repeatedly.

"Cut. It. Out," Paul says to us, giving me a kick in the ribs, hard enough for me to loosen my grip on my younger brother. "We gotta clean your back. Come on."

Samuel coughs and takes a deep breath as I stand up, wincing from my back and my bleeding tongue.

"You're such a fart-knocker," he says, grabbing the stair railing. "One of these days you won't be able to do that anymore, Danny."

I grin, looking at Johnny. "We'll see about that."

Johnny smirks as I walk into the bathroom after Paul, looking in the toothpaste-splattered mirror. Crimson shines on my teeth and I spit into the sink as Paul gets out the peroxide and Neosporin. Around here, we go through this shit like candy on Halloween.

"Warn me bef— OUCH," I say, jerking away from him. "Dude!"

"My bad." He chuckles. "You got some major road rash."

Samuel stands at the doorway. "That's what you get for being an idiot."

I reach my hand out to grab him, but Paul yanks my arm as Samuel stumbles backward and falls on his butt. "Will you two stop?" Paul barks.

I grin because my little brother is on his ass. He gets up, sticking his tongue out at me.

I wince when Paul pours more peroxide onto my back. Straightening my spine and arms, I ball my fists. This isn't the first time I've fallen on the skateboard, but it's the first time I fell because of a person.

Bexley Walker has stumbled into our lives out of nowhere. I think about a few nights ago when I was sitting on the roof watching the house burn and the firemen do their best to try to stop it. I wondered when they would discover Johnny's dad was in there.

I wondered what his body smelled like as his skin sizzled, and then I saw her run out of the house next door. She looked upset. When she took off running, I only had one thought.

Where is she going?

Genesis

And she shouldn't be running off alone in this neighborhood.

Don't ask me why I gave a shit. I still don't know the answer to that. But she seemed like she had the whole world on her shoulders. Like whatever she was tore up about was life-changing.

She'll be in Samuel's grade. I wonder if she goes to church, and how that cut is on her jaw.

It'll be a scar for sure, just like the many I have.

It shocked me stupid that she didn't jump up and burst into tears. I've never seen a girl not cry after getting hurt. The girls at school are wimps. They fall and scrape their knee and whine like someone broke their arm.

I feel the slickness of Neosporin as Paul rubs it across my skin.

"You can't sleep on your back tonight," Paul says.

"Duh," I reply. Paul's like the father figure around here. He gets on my nerves, though, always telling us what to do.

Paul replaces the top back on the medicine and washes his hands before drying them on a towel.

"You three wash up and put shirts on." He exits the bathroom and Samuel and I fight over who's washing their hands first while Johnny chooses to wash his in the tub.

Paige P. Horne

We sit at the table as Ma places the pan of spaghetti down onto the flowery tablecloth. The wooden chair creaks when she takes a seat and she looks at us expectedly. We all bow our heads and take each other's hands as she begins grace.

"Bless us, O God, as we sit together. Bless the food we eat today. Bless the hands that made the food. Bless us, O God. Amen."

We each make the sign of the cross and say, "Amen."

"Did you boys see the new neighbors we have?" Ma asks as she grabs the pan and starts loading up our plates.

"Yes, ma'am," Paul says.

She nods. "I've got a cake baking in the oven. "You'll take it over when it's done," she says, looking at all of us.

I look over at Johnny who's also looking at me. "Yes, ma'am," we all say.

"Good boys. Wipe your mouth, Samuel," she says. My younger brother lifts his napkin and wipes his mouth. My shirt's sticking to my back and it's uncomfortable.

Genesis

"Danny hit the new neighbor on the skateboard," Samuel says. I kick his leg under the table, glowering at him. He doesn't say anything as I look over at Ma.

"Don't speak with your mouth full," she says to him and then points her eyes on me. "Danny, how did you do that?"

"I was coming down the hill. She got in my way."

She narrows her eyes at me. "Are you hurt?"

I shrug. "Just my back."

"Do I need to look at it?" she asks me.

"I cleaned it up," Paul chimes in, wiping his own mouth.

She nods. "Good." She lifts her fork, twirling the pasta. "I assume you apologized?"

Crap.

"Umm, well, not really."

"Danny O'Brien. You will apologize to that girl when you take the cake over. You four will make her feel welcome in this neighborhood. You know what it's like to be the new kid. It's no fun."

I frown, looking down at my food. I should have lied. "Yes, ma'am," I say.

"Good. Now finish your dinner. It's your turn to do the dishes."

Paige P. Horne

I groan inwardly but continue to eat. Ma's hair is transforming from brown to gray, and the skin around her eyes is wrinkling more each day. We lived a few streets over from Ma and Pa when my parents were alive, but they never came to visit, so my brothers and I would walk to visit them. Pa didn't like our dad. Paul says he didn't want Mom to marry him.

Supposedly, Dad was a bad man, but what's a bad man? He made money; he provided for his family. So what, he didn't go to a nine-to-five job every day? He got his hands a little dirty, and to me that was okay. I was a cactus around our dad and retained the advice he used to give me like water.

"Just because you want to live a different way than the rest doesn't mean you're the bad person. Maybe the motherfucker sitting at his desk job getting blowed by his receptionist before he goes home to the wifey is the bad person. I feel sorry for blokes like that. They're stuck."

I'd sit on the floor in his office when I was just a little kid and play with toy cars. Dad had business guys come in and they'd talk about whatever it was they had going on. I heard things like *bookie* and *shylock*. I didn't know what those words meant, but I was pretty sure my dad was a bookie.

Genesis

The guys called him "Pen" I'm assuming 'cause he always had a pen and notebooks in front of him. He always had the TV on sports and the phones were always ringing. Our house was busy, and it was always the same people moving in and out.

Our dad was the coolest. I looked up to him. He made his way of living seem fun. Who the hell wants to slide into a pair of slacks every day to go to a dead-end job that'll only get you so much in life?

Our parents' death was hard to handle. I still can't shake Mom's eyes while those men climbed on top of her. But it's not fear I felt. It was rage. I was hiding in the closet, and Paul and Samuel snuck out the window, leaving me to witness our parents' death.

Dad came home late from work and caught them. He fought hard, but in the end a bullet won. Both of their souls were taken right before my eyes. I knew right then my life would forever be changed and not because I no longer had parents, but in a different way.

I saw evil up close and it slithered its way past the hinges that held up the door I was hiding behind. It crawled—a cloud as black as charcoal under the gap I was looking out of with my cheek pressed against the dusty floor.

Paige P. Horne

I felt it when it wrapped around my veins, snaking and fusing itself to me. That was the first time I had the urge to kill. And while it should have been a traumatic moment for a little kid, to me it was a lesson.

Don't be the losing guy.

I don't know why my parents were murdered, but right after it happened, I found myself outside in the yard surround by cops, being questioned about what I saw. I was like a deer in the headlights, standing there with blood on my hands and a shake in my bones that wouldn't go away.

I wasn't talking to them. I was staring at my brothers who were sitting on the steps, looking just like me, and then a car drove up and a man got out. He walked into the yard like he owned the place.

The cop that was talking to me stopped and went to him. Some words I couldn't hear were exchanged. The cop looked back at me, and then he walked away from the guy in the suit. I was then approached.

"You're Pen's boy, right?"

I nodded.

"You know what the men who did this looked like?"

I nodded again.

Genesis

"Don't talk to these cops. We take care of our own around here. Once they all leave, you come down to where I'm located. You know the place?" he asked.

"Yes," I said.

"Yes, sir," he replied.

"Yes, sir."

"Good. Meet me down there."

I did as the man asked, and after some weeks had passed, while sitting on the couch one evening, I saw on the news that a family was murdered. The man of the family? The same man who took my parents' life.

A few days later, while leaving the corner store with a Coke and a candy bar, I was approached again by this man.

"Listen, kid. I had respect for your old man. He was a good guy. Loyal. And your mom was a good woman. Rest your head knowing their death was avenged."

And it was then I knew. He took care of the people who killed my family. He then pulled out a card from his black suit jacket. "You ever need anything, you give Moretti a call."

I took the card and he ruffled my hair before walking off. I watched as he strolled away and the two men with him followed like loyal dogs. I looked after them with a certain wonder until they all got into a car and sped off. I got the idea that this Moretti dude was in charge and the guys with him had his back. I remember wanting that.

I wanted what Moretti had.

I also remember thinking… *these guys are gangsters.*

And maybe I wanted that, too.

Chapter Seven
Danny
1998

Samuel holds on to the cake as Paul knocks on the door. Moments later, a woman swings it open. She's tiny, her hair is dark, and there are bald spots on top. She touches her head, looking a little embarrassed. I look over at Paul who slightly shakes his head, meaning *don't say anything*. Quickly, she reaches over, grabs a black beanie, and slides it over her hair.

"Boys?" she says. "Can I help you?"

"Yes, ma'am. I'm Paul, and this is Samuel, Danny, and Johnny." Paul slides his hands into his pockets. "We live next door. This cake is a welcome-to-the-neighborhood gift from our grandmother."

"Oh," she says with a smile in her tone. "How nice." She reaches for the cake. "I'm Cora Walker." She turns around and places it on a table before looking back at us and wrapping her gray sweater around her small frame. "I'll get Bexley to run the cake holder back to you."

"Thanks," Paul says. He clears his throat. "Um, Danny and Bexley got into a little accident earlier. He needs to apologize."

"Oh," she says in a that's-what-happened way. "Yes, she has a nasty cut on her jaw." She looks at me, not like I'm in trouble, but like this is cute that I want to say I'm sorry.

She's judging this situation wrong. I have no desire to apologize.

Paul nudges me. "Sorry about that," I say.

Mrs. Walker tries to hide her smile. "Kids will be kids," she replies. She opens the door wider and turns around. "Bexley," she calls out.

I study Mrs. Walker as she looks to the stairs. She's pretty. Would be prettier if her cheeks weren't sunken in and her eyes were a little brighter. She looks like she's sick, dying even, and now I think I know why Bexley Walker was so upset the other night.

Moments later, the girl I have to apologize to walks down the stairs. She's got headphones from a Walkman hooked around her neck.

"Yeah, Mom?" she says but stops when she sees us, pointing her eyes at me mostly.

"This young man wants to say something to you," Mrs. Walker says.

Genesis

Bexley looks apprehensive as she slowly starts to walk again. She looks to her mom when she hits the bottom step.

"Come here," Mrs. Walker urges her daughter.

Bexley walks over until she's standing in front of us with a lifted brow. Like we're intruding on her music time or something.

"Sorry about earlier," I say, looking at the bandage she wears on her chin.

"Okay," she says. I smirk because I can't help it. I just apologized and she has shit to say about it. No *I'm sorry, too.* Or *I should have been paying better attention.* Granted, I also should have been paying better attention, but still.

No one here but Johnny knows we've already met, and no one knows at all that we busted out windows just a few nights ago.

Bexley and I have secrets and we've only known each other a few days.

And I like that about us.

"You don't have anything to say?" I ask her.

Paul kicks the back of my foot and Mrs. Walker narrows her eyes at her kid.

"Nope," Bexley says with a shrug. "Can I go back now?" she asks her mom.

"Don't you think you should say thank you?" Mrs. Walker asks her.

I was going for she's sorry, too, but okay.

It's not very noticeable, but I catch it when Bexley's jaw tightens. Her fist balls for only a moment. She's angry.

She turns to me. "Thanks," she says as politely as she can muster. But I taste the bitterness of it on my tongue and I have a strong urge to laugh, but I don't.

She's different than the girls at school. Tougher, like life's already shown her its bad side, too.

I like that about her.

"Yeah," I reply. "No problem."

"All right then," Paul says. "Nice meeting you. Enjoy the cake."

"Thanks again," Mrs. Walker says as we four descend the steps.

"Good going," Paul says to me.

"What?" I ask. "The girl's an asshole."

"And you're not?" he throws back.

I shrug, trying to hide the smile on my face. "Come on, Johnny. Let's go."

"Better be home before dark," Paul says as he and Samuel climb the stoop to our house. Samuel looks between Johnny and me, disappointment on his face.

"We'll be back later, man," I tell him. He nods and Johnny and I head across the street.

Genesis

Once out of my brothers' vision, I slip out a pack of cigarettes and hand him one.

"You all right?" I ask him.

He nods. "Fine."

Johnny doesn't talk much, but it's what makes what he says important when he does.

He pulls out his Zippo lighter and lights the smoke before handing it over to me. I run my thumb across the front like he did when he took it from his father.

"Think the girl will keep her mouth shut?" he asks.

I nod. "She has so far." I don't tell Johnny about her and me the other night. For some reason, I just feel like it's no one's business.

He looks back in front of him.

"Think Moretti can help me with this foster home shit?" he asks as we cross the road, hitting the sidewalk.

"He told me if I ever needed anything to give him a call," I reply with a smile as I light my own cigarette. I hand him back his lighter, catching his own smile. I knew the point of this was to help Johnny with his new situation, but to me this was going to mean more.

Paige P. Horne

Taking help from Moretti meant we owed him something in return. I wasn't stupid in that matter, and truthfully, I didn't care.

I've wanted Moretti's way of living ever since he told me he offed the people who killed my parents.

And this was my way in.

Chapter Eight
Danny
2003

Buses with black smoke roll down the streets as kids with no home training play on the sidewalks. We turn left, and as soon as we stop, I reach in the back, taking hold of the iron wrench and pulling at the bottom of my hoodie as I hop out of my 1996 Impala.

"Hey, white boy, this isn't your side of town."

I smile at the man who's at least seven feet tall. He doesn't know it, but his face is about to be fucked up. With Johnny at my back, I jump up, removing the wrench at the same time. As I swing my arm upward, the hard iron meets his face and I hear bones crush. It brings him to his knees, and I continue slamming into his head while he tries to cover himself.

Blood splatters and I wipe my sleeve across my forehead. His boy runs out of the store, and Johnny takes care of him as the man in front of me slumps down.

"May the cat eat you and the devil eat the cat." I spit beside him. "Tell Warren this is his last warning. Get off our streets." I signal for Johnny to come on. I toss the iron wrench in the back floorboard and we climb into the Impala and ride out.

Passing run-down streets and buildings that need an update, I grab a smoke and run my hand through my hair. "Fucking Warren and his crew selling cut heroine on our street corner. He knows that's against the rules. He's giving these people dope that's mostly latex, underselling Moretti so they'll buy from him instead. So, when they do buy from Moretti, they're doubling up their dose and fucking overdosing. It's a shit show."

"He doesn't give a shit," Johnny says.

"Well, he's fucking with the wrong people."

"I know," Johnny says. "But you know what we did back there is going to come with repercussions."

"Let them motherfuckers come," I say.

"Yo, Danny," someone yells and I lift my chin at a group of kids as I light my cigarette. Time has a way of changing you. Time has a way of changing everything.

It's been five years since we burned down Johnny's house. Five years of growing up and understanding more about the streets.

After we walked into Moretti's shop, things started to change for Johnny and me. We told him about Johnny's situation.

"You burned the man up in the house?" Moretti asked.

"Yeah," Johnny replied with his hands in his pockets.

I remember the hard look Moretti had on his face, and then he looked at the two men who occupied the room with us. Out of nowhere they all started laughing.

I didn't know what was so damn funny, and the way Johnny looked at me, he didn't either.

But the look on Moretti's face was pride. He was proud of us.

"You two got some balls," he said. "Wouldn't you say, Nugget?" he asked one of the men at the door.

This guy had a gold tooth right in the center of his mouth. It's like his teeth were all out of whack or something and he was always smiling, which made it stand out even more. The joke was the tooth was so big it looked like an actual gold nugget, hence the nickname.

We were never alone with Moretti. There were always at least two men inside his office with suits on just like him. Shiny shoes and gold rings on their fingers. They never wore the same suit twice. It fucking amazed me. I wanted that type of money. I wanted that kind of life.

I didn't invent the type of world where gangsters ruled the streets and carried thick bills in their pockets, but hell, if I was going to live in it, I was going to have my fucking share. If this meant climbing a ladder, stepping on top of a few people while going up, then so be it.

"I'd say," Nugget replied to Moretti. "How old are you kids, anyway?"

"Thirteen," I spoke up.

"Geesh," the other guy said, more to himself.

He was taller than Nugget. His hair was turning silver and it didn't match his face. He seemed too young for gray hair.

"How'd you do it?" Moretti asked us.

"Moonshine," I replied.

He lifted his brow. "Moonshine?"

"Yes, sir," Johnny said.

"Where the hell did you get moonshine?"

"My old man only drank homemade moonshine. He meets a man near Scotts Mountain to supply up. Well, he did," he said. "He's got a shitload of it out in the shed. I figured since he loved it so much, he could burn up in it."

The three men looked at each other, and the silver haired one lifted his brow. Johnny sounded like a psychopath, but he wasn't. He was just a boy who'd had enough of his father beating him every day.

Genesis

They say it's the quiet ones you have to worry about, and Johnny was always quiet. They also say there's only so much a person can take before they fucking explode.

Well, Johnny exploded and I helped light the fuse—happily, I might add.

"So, what are you here for?" Moretti asked, looking back at us as he linked his digits.

"Johnny no longer has a parent. Social services are coming to get him."

"And you don't want that?" he asked, looking at Johnny.

"No. I want to stay with Danny."

Nugget spoke up. "What are you two? Butch Cassidy and the Sundance Kid? Look at these little fuckers, Mickey." He laughed.

Mickey was the one with the silver hair. I wanted to knock Nugget's shiny tooth out and shove it down his throat, but I was smaller than him, and I knew if I stuck around, there would come a time for that. I don't usually forget little things like his smart-ass remark.

And believe me when I say, I can hold a fucking grudge better than anyone. You cross me or my boy Johnny, you'll pay for it.

It may not be right then, but trust me, I'll come for you.

Mickey didn't return Nugget's laugh, and that made me have some respect for him. But Nugget lost my respect at that very moment.

I think I'm a pretty fair guy. I don't look at people like they're shit before I get to know them. You have to show me you're shit, and then I don't forget it.

It's simple, really. Show me who you are, and I'll believe you.

"Okay. I'll see what I can do about that." Moretti leaned back. "But I need you to do something for me," he said.

"Anything," I replied.

I felt Johnny look at me like I just signed my soul over to the fallen angel himself, but what Johnny failed to realize was *I* was the devil. Moretti was just helping me become who I was meant to be.

"Get me in contact with the man who makes that moonshine. You boys are going to start selling it to these alcoholics that run the streets. I'll under sale the liquor stores, and eventually they'll want to come to me for business."

I looked at Johnny, asking without asking if that was an issue.

He nodded slightly.

Genesis

"Yes, sir," I said to Moretti.

"Good. Come back when you have the connection. I'll work on this little social services issue."

"Thank you," I said, and we headed to the door.

"By the way," he said as we walked out. "I'm proud of you. You took control of a shitty situation. You changed your own outcome. There's something to be said about that."

I nodded, and before I stepped through the door, I looked at Nugget. "Nice tooth," I told him.

"Thanks, Sundance Kid." He winked at me, and I smiled, and not because I was happy, but because I knew, one day, he'd no longer have that fucking tooth or a beating heart.

On top of doing the moonshine, we did little things like ran errands. Moretti didn't like doing business over the phone, so Johnny and I would run all over the neighborhood delivering his messages. We also got his dry cleaning and cleaned up the beer bottles and cigarette butts in the courtyard behind his shop.

In exchange, we got some cash in our pocket and more times than not, we got to have a beer or two. Plus, we got to learn the business. It was a win-win for us, and we knew eventually it would turn into something more.

We were becoming one of them. In a world where we didn't belong, we'd found somewhere we did.

I don't know what Moretti did, but he got it worked out where Johnny could at least stay in the neighborhood. Which was good enough, I guess. The guy Johnny was staying with only cared about the check he was getting every month for keeping him, so Johnny mostly stayed with us anyway. He only had to go home when child services came around.

Life was fucking good, man. Before we knew it, a year had flown by, and the more time that passed, the more things Moretti let us in on. Mickey James was his right-hand man. He'd take us on runs. We'd go around the neighborhood and collect payments for keeping the local businesses safe. He did the dirty work for Moretti, which meant taking another's life if he crossed any of us.

The shit we saw, no other fourteen-year-old was seeing. You got folks who walk around really thinking this world is a good place, but it's only good to certain people.

The ones on top.

Genesis

Johnny and I were wearing all the latest clothes and the coolest shoes. Paul was curious at times, asked us how we were getting all the stuff we had. We lied, of course, telling him the guy Johnny was living with was letting us help him flip houses.

It gave us reason to be gone all day. He was too busy with school anyway to really dig into it, so he let it go most of the time. Ma didn't pay any attention. She stayed in church and played bridge on the weekends.

Samuel stayed to himself a lot as we got older. He went to school like he was supposed to and had his own small group of friends he hung out with. He played baseball and met some boys from the north side.

Eventually, he convinced Ma to let him switch schools. He used his friend's address so he could attend. We were once a tight-knit family, but things never stay the same.

"Stop the car," I say to Johnny. He does without question and I lean out the window. "You boys should be in school," I say to the kids standing on the corner.

"Come on. We know you never went to school," one kid with a smoke behind his ear says.

"Don't be like me," I say. "Get your asses to school and toss that cigarette." I lean back inside the car and look over at Johnny. "Fucking kids."

Johnny doesn't say anything as he hits the gas.

They're not wrong, though. School was never my thing, and I hardly went. I wanted to make money, and I knew that didn't include a boring ass nine-to-five. So, I dropped out when I turned sixteen. Ma wasn't happy, but she didn't stop me.

I've always been a street kid. I learned that life isn't always easy, but if you're in charge, it can be.

Johnny seemed to go with whatever I wanted, but this lifestyle wasn't a choice for me. It's in my blood to be different than the rest. My dad was, and I would be, too. Not all men were meant to wear a suit and tie and clock in every day, but that didn't mean I wasn't going to have to work hard.

One thing my dad always said was, *"You've got to do your own growing, no matter how tall your father was."* Success is never guaranteed.

I knew from a young age if I stayed close to the right people, I would learn everything I wanted to know. I put myself around the best of them. Kingpins and gangsters. Now I'm talking real gangsters, not the kind with baggy pants and a sideways pointed gun. I'm talking about the men in tailored suits who will put you six feet under for smarting off to them at the dinner table.

Genesis

I'm talking men who don't have to get blood on their hands because they have people who do it for them.

I'm those people.

You don't get to where I am by being clean. Johnny's old man isn't the only person we've put in the ground. We've taken care of two people who've wronged Moretti. One thing you've got to learn is, it's just business. There's nothing personal about this shit.

You do someone wrong, you pay for it, and most of the time it's with your life. Growing up in the rough streets of Postings, New Jersey will teach you that.

I'm not proud of the things I've done. I'm not a good man, but in this lifestyle, you have to make shit decisions, and sometimes it's kill or be killed. I've earned my place here more than once, and I've gained respect by giving it.

"Let's get to Ma's," I say to Johnny. "I'm starving, and you know what they say."

He looks over at me with a lifted brow.

"Hunger is good sauce." I laugh, hitting Mr. Uptight on the chest. "It's Thanksgiving, Johnny. Be a little fucking happy, would ya?"

He looks back at the road and I flip the sun visor down, wiping the blood off my cheek, but it's still on my hands. We pull up to the curb, seeing Ma heading into the house with an arm full of groceries. Johnny parks the car and we both hop out.

"Ma, we got that," I say. "Johnny, grab a few bags, would ya?" I hit my smoke one hard time before tossing it as I run up to the porch so I can get the door.

I hold it open with my body, sliding my hands into my hoodie's pockets and turning to see Samuel walking down the stairs. "You knew Ma was coming home. Help with the bags," I tell him, blowing smoke away from the door so it doesn't get into her house. Ma used to smoke, but she doesn't anymore.

"Shit," he says, running over to the door. "I didn't know she'd be back so quickly."

"You shouldn't smoke those, Danny," Ma says as she pats my arm.

"I shouldn't do a lot of things, Ma. Go on inside," I tell her. I grab Samuel now that his hands are full and dig my knuckles into his skull. "What's up, north side punk?" I say.

"Fuck, Danny, get off," he says, ducking away from me.

"Hey, watch your language in front of Ma," I tell him, looking up when I see someone at the top of the stairs.

Holy shit. She bites her bottom lip, looking a bit shy. Her hair is pulled back and her cheeks are flushed.

Genesis

Wait.

"You remember Bexley," Samuel says, walking past me with the some more groceries.

Johnny follows Ma toward the kitchen. "What can I help you with?" he asks her. I hear the bags being placed onto the countertop, and I look from Bexley to my brother, noticing his hair is wet and taking in the fact he smelled like body wash when he walked by. He just got out of the shower. He's been upstairs messing around with Bexley Walker. Something fires inside my chest.

The one I used to call Little Girl has grown up.

Good God has she grown up. It's been what? Three years now since I've seen her.

I remember the blood on my hands, and I take off up the steps, not looking away from her once round, childlike face. It's thinned out. Her breasts are full, her neck slender. Her eyes widen the closer I get, and if I remember correctly, there are flecks of gold in them. She stays in place, not moving.

"You fucking my brother?" I ask, seeing a faint glimpse of the scar I put on her jaw when we were kids. Memories of crashing into a human wall flip through my mind.

She narrows her eyes at me. "Hey to you, too," she says.

I smirk, giving her a once-over. I step, making her back up. She tilts her head, looking at the side of my face.

"Is that blood?" she asks. My facial expression doesn't change. She crosses her arms, her shirt riding up, showing off skin. Skin I'd like to touch.

"I see you haven't changed."

I smile. "I am who I am, Little Girl."

She lifts her brow at the nickname I used to call her. "I'm not a little girl anymore, Danny."

My eyes dart down. "I see that."

Something ignites in the air around us. A tension that's always been there. After we crashed into each other on the street all those years ago, Bexley became part of the family. Paul took her in, and Samuel clearly had a crush. However, there was something more with us two.

But I was older, into different things, and she was Little Girl. I've always been taller than her, but now I tower over her small frame. We each study one another, taking in things we've forgotten over the years and things that have changed. The scars have faded, the kid in us gone.

She's right. She isn't a little girl anymore, and I'm not the same rough kid. The feelings might still be there, but I see who she's chosen.

"You should get downstairs," I say, stepping around her. Once in the bathroom, I push the door to, but not without a quick glance at Bexley. She exhales and holds on to the stair railing, her head pointed toward the floor. She shakes it, lifts her chin, and heads down to my brother.

Chapter Nine

Bexley
Two days missing

I've been floating. Floating for hours. Whatever the stranger gave me has me drifting in and out, and my body feels like I weigh a thousand pounds, but my head, God, my head feels as light as a feather. He came by sometime in the night and forced water down our throats, along with a few pieces of bread, but that's hardly satisfying, and I believe there were only more drugs in whatever he gave us.

"Are you up?"

I wince when I move my head. "Yeah."

"Are you okay?"

"No," I say weakly.

"Are you hurt, Bexley? I need to know if…"

"I'm not hurt, Danny. Not physically, just my head. He's drugged me."

"He's drugged us both," he says.

"Who is he?"

"I don't know, but he says he knows me."

I scoff. "Of course, he does."

"What does that mean?" he asks.

I laugh bitterly. "It just means I'm not surprised, Danny." He doesn't respond, and I shut my eyes tightly, tilting my head to the ceiling. My heart is frozen over, but just being in the same room with him, I feel it start to thaw and I hate myself for it. We have so much history between us, but we've grown cold toward one another, or I have, with good reason.

This man came into my life as a boy, and I fell so hopelessly in love with him, only to be destroyed by his way of living. I tried to get away from it all, I tried to move on, but that's the thing about Danny. He's never truly let me go.

"I'm sorry, Bexley. You don't know how sorry I am."

"I'm sure I have an idea," I say, unenthused. I've heard his apologies one too many times. It changes nothing. I exhale slowly as the sound of rain falls outside, hammering on the roof above us. I still have no idea where we are. There's no outside noise, no cars, no people, nothing. We have no way to keep up with time, besides the light.

"How long have we been here?" I ask.

"A couple of days, I believe."

"Do you remember what happened?" I ask. "We were attacked, right?"

"Yeah, we were heading to the shop and someone jumped us from behind. He hit me in the head with the grip of a gun, I believe."

"You got back up, though. You were fighting him."

"Well, I lost." He winces.

Genesis

"Are you okay?" I ask, concerned, and instantly hating that I didn't cover it better.

"Just sore. Don't worry about me." I hear the amusement in his voice.

"Who said I was worried?" I shift in my chair, my ass hurting from being in this same position for so long.

"You asked, Bexley, and I know when you're worried."

"You don't know me anymore, Danny."

"So what? You think because you went off and got married you've changed so much? That I don't know who you are anymore? That's ridiculous."

My heart drops when I think about my husband, and I can't help the pain that slides down my cheek. I sniff, wishing I was alone, if only for a moment so I could let this grief out inside my chest. It's so heavy, so goddamn heavy.

"So, there was only one man then?" Danny asks, changing the subject, and I hate that he probably knows I'm crying.

I inhale a shaky breath. "I think. That's all I saw anyway. I jumped on his back, but it was useless. I don't really know what happened after that."

"You jumped on his back?" he asks, and I hear amusement again in his smug voice.

"He was kicking you in the ribs. What else was I going to do?"

He chuckles, wincing after he does. This time I don't ask if he's okay. I realize that his ribs are bruised if not broken. I wonder about his other injuries. He was hit on the head. I hope he's not sitting here bleeding.

God, why do I care?

He's the reason we're here in the first place. He's the reason my life has gone to shit.

I look up. Will we ever get out of here? How did this happen? Who is this man, and what does he want with us?

"Do you remember the first time we saw each other again after you moved away?" he asks.

See? He never let me go. Hence, why I'm fucking here. I don't understand what is wrong with me. I shouldn't have even been with him, but he assured me I was in danger.

I laugh to myself; he wasn't wrong.

"Don't," I reply. "I'm not doing this with you."

He's hurt me too much. He doesn't get to sit here and reminisce about old days.

"You act as if you had no part in any of the bad we experienced," he tosses back.

I sneer. "You really want to point fingers right now?"

"I want you to admit that you're not Miss Perfect in this fucking situation."

"Fuck you, Danny. How about you not talk to me and I won't talk to you?"

Genesis

"Fine," he says.

"Fine," I reply. I move my wrists, wishing I could untie them. My breath comes out ragged, and I look toward where I think Danny is.

His words replay in my mind. *"Do you remember the first time we saw each other again after you moved away?"*

Of course, I remember. How could I not? Seeing Danny again after so long was a highlight in my life. Who knew where it would lead at the time.

I surely didn't or I would have run.

Chapter Ten
Bexley
2003

I hit the bottom step, walking into the living room, which I completely bypassed when I first got here. Nostalgia hits me like a ton of bricks. I'm catapulted back to 1998. Ma hasn't done much with the place. It looks exactly the same as it did when I was a kid. Same couch, same outdated TV, and same small wooden coffee table with the white polyester lace table runner.

Before Mama died and I had no choice but to move across town to live with my uncle Hale, I was in this house more than once after I met the O'Brien boys. Truthfully, I loved being here. Ma always made me feel welcome, and being here gave me some reprieve from being around sickness and the daily reminder of death.

After I witnessed the boys burning down Johnny's house, we never mentioned it again. It was like I had some special secret with the two. Paul eventually came around to me hanging out with them. One day he just decided I was part of the family. He always invited me to eat with them and was constantly watching my back at school.

Genesis

It was nice having more family than just my mama and uncle. And the night my mama died, I never needed my new extended family more.

Bexley
Year 2000

"She's not in any pain," the nurse tells me as I sit by Mama's side holding her fragile hand. Her chest shudders, and it terrifies me. I look down at her digits slipped in between mine. How small they seem for a woman who was so strong. She lived longer than they thought. My chest clenches in agony.

I'm losing her.

I look out the window, a feeling as heavy as an ocean wave crashing down on top of me passes through my soul.

Despair.

Heartache.

Pain so severe I can taste it.

Why do our minds replay all the special memories we shared with a person when they die? Why do I remember all the good things about my mama? It only hurts worse. Moments of laughter, of her picking me up when I fell. I see her smile behind my eyes, her sweet scent after she's just left a room.

Paige P. Horne

The sound of her humming while she's cooking pancakes on a Sunday morning.

I die inside.

Loaded with pain, I feel salty tears slip from my eyes, crawling down my cheeks. Mama takes a deep breath. My eyes go to her chest and I watch it fall, but it moves no more. I hang my head, close my eyes, and let my heart rip in two. My whole body shakes. I kiss her hand before leaning up and kissing her cheek, and then I reach around her neck and remove the locket she always wears. A photo of us lives inside.

"No matter where I go, or what I do, I'll never, never forget you." I cry. "What will I do without you?" My chest quakes, my vison blurry. I place the locket around my neck, squeeze Mama's hand one more time, and then I walk out. Uncle Hale looks up when I exit the room. My eyes go to the clock on the wall. Ten minutes after nine.

"She's gone," I say.

He looks down, his own grief washing over him.

"I'm sorry, kid," he says.

I sniff. "Can I go next door?" I ask.

He nods. "Yeah, sure."

I walk past him and head out the door, running over to the boys' house. I knock three times and Ma answers. I don't have to say anything. They all knew this was happening.

Genesis

"I'm so sorry," she says, grabbing me in a hug. She pulls me into the house. "Is your uncle over there?"

I nod, unable to speak.

"I'll give him a call. You'll stay here tonight, if that's what you want?"

I nod again. Paul and Samuel sit in the living room. Paul's dressed, clearly going out. He stands up with his keys in his hand. "Sorry, Bex," he says, giving me his own hug. He smells like cologne and aftershave. At seventeen, Paul's fading more and more away from this neighborhood. I want that for him. He's like the older brother I never had, and I love him so much.

"You take my room," he says. "The sheets are clean." He gives me a wink and I give him a weak smile in thanks. "I'll be back later, Ma," he adds, heading out the door.

"Be safe," she replies. I look over at Samuel. He's the same age as me and just as cute as his brothers.

"You wanna watch a movie or something?" he asks. I wonder where Danny, the boy who followed me in the dark when I found out Mama's cancer had spread, is right now. The boy who stopped coming to my window and made my heart almost combust with happiness on my thirtieth birthday, only to break it when he wouldn't stay the night with me.

Paige P. Horne

He's never home anymore, and I miss him. I miss the sound of tiny rocks tapping on my bedroom window. I miss hearing about his wild nights running the streets. We grew so close. He's heard my mama's coughing fits. He's been there when I've tried not to cry because she was spitting up blood. The only thing I really don't miss is when he used to tell me about his girlfriends at school. It made my stomach burn.

Disappointment is nothing new when I think of Danny. I'm sure he's only thought of me as a little girl and that's why he's always called me that. Of course, he isn't here the night my mama dies. Danny has a one-track mind when it comes to the streets.

He wants to own them. At only fifteen, the boy I like is into some bad stuff.

"Yeah," I say to Samuel. "A movie sounds good."

Ma makes us some popcorn, but I don't touch it. Samuel and I sit on opposite ends of the couch, and after Ma goes to bed, we stay that way. Samuel is the good brother. He does his homework and stays out of trouble. He's nothing like his two older brothers.

Paul is smart, and his mind is always working. He's a good guy on the outside, but you can tell there's something inside of him he doesn't show to everyone. It's his best kept secret.

Genesis

Danny doesn't hide anything. He shows you exactly who he is. He's straightforward and that sometimes hurts, but it's him. The church clock chimes, telling us it's past midnight now. Samuel has tried to make me laugh. He's sweet, but my heart isn't happy, and when your heart is sad, it affects everything.

"I'm going to go on up," I tell him. "Thanks for hanging out with me."

"Anytime," he says. His brown hair falls in front of his eyes and he swipes it out of the way. "I'm really sorry about your mom. I know…" He takes in a breath. "I know it hurts, but it will get easier."

"I hope so. This is rough," I say sadly.

"Yeah. Goodnight, Bex."

"Goodnight."

After I shut Paul's bedroom door, I slide down it and let the tears fall. I hold on to Mama's locket and beg for her to talk to me. Show me she's not gone forever, but that never comes. Eventually, I get off the floor and remove my jeans. I slide under the comforter and sheets, staring out the window.

From here you can hear the cargo ships' horns from the Delaware, proving that the world is moving on without my mom.

It hurts.

And as I finally drift off to sleep, I hear the door open. I smell his scent and hear his shoes kick off, and then he climbs over me. Danny gets under the covers with me, and if I wasn't so hurt, I'd probably stop him, but right now I need the comfort. I need to know I'm not dying, too.

He wraps his arm around my stomach, but I turn to him, snaking my hand over his waist and around his back. I grip his shirt and weep into his chest. He holds me, and I cry myself to sleep, knowing I'm not alone.

I shake my head slightly, feeling the pain of that evening in my chest, as though it just happened. I was mostly crying because I'd just lost my mom, but a small part of me was crying because it had been so long since I'd been close to the boy I secretly loved. After that, I was sent off to live with my uncle Hale who lived in the nicer part of town. I went to a different school and sadly, I lost touch with the O'Brien boys, but that doesn't mean they weren't on my mind. I was so happy when Samuel switched schools a few months ago and I ran into him in the hallway.

The boy who watched a movie with me the night my mom died has become an important person in my life. We've grown close.

I head into the dining room to get to the kitchen where everyone but Danny is. God, how much he's changed since the last time I saw him. He's rougher, meaner.

And breathtaking.

Genesis

I know I shouldn't like the boy who walked into the house with blood on his face, but honestly, the bad side of Danny is what turns me on.

And I'm not ashamed to admit that.

"Can I help?" I ask.

"Bexley Walker," Ma says with a big smile on her face. "Oh, my goodness." She walks over to me, giving me a huge hug. I breathe in comfort and childhood memories. I know it's only been five years, but a lot can change in that amount of time.

Like Ma here. She's grown older, grayer, and her face isn't as smooth as it once was. But she's Ma and I've missed her so much.

She pulls away, her eyes scanning over me. "My goodness, you've grown. Such a beautiful young woman." She turns to the boys. "Isn't she?" she says.

"Yep," Samuel says.

I smile at her, slightly blushing. "Thank you." Samuel walks over to me, grabbing my hand. I look over at Johnny who leans against the counter.

"How have you been, Johnny?"

He nods. "Fine."

"Good," I reply. Johnny and Danny have always been close. I guess that's one other thing that hasn't changed.

Danny walks into the kitchen, heading to the fridge. I see his eyes dart down to mine and

Samuel's hands, but it doesn't seem to affect him. He grabs a beer from the fridge.

"Danny, you know you shouldn't drink," Ma says, walking over to the sink to wash her hands.

"And you shouldn't dip that snuff either, Ma, but we don't call you out." He winks at her.

She grins. "Touché."

Ma's always just let the boys do their own thing. She's said, *"As long as you stay out of trouble and be smart, then I have no problems."*

Danny twists off the top of his beer. "Let's go, Johnny."

My heart drops to the pit of my stomach with disappointment.

He's now in a black T-shirt with faded jeans, his hair is wet from the shower he just had, and as he walks by me, my knees weaken and butterflies soar. God, he's something. I've dreamed about him for years. How I wished he'd throw rocks at my window again and want to climb inside.

How much I've wanted to show him I'm not that little girl anymore, but perfectly capable of matching up to him.

But he never came to visit and neither did I. He clearly doesn't see me any differently from when I left. Samuel and I have been spending a lot of time together, but we're not official or anything. I love being around him, and he's soul-shatteringly kind.

But there's no hard rush.

Genesis

There's no out-of-control beating from my chest. Regardless, I care about him. I always have.

I hear the front door open. "Where are you going?"

I smile hearing that voice.

"Well, look what the cat dragged in," Danny says, and I can hear the happy in his tone.

I let go of Samuel's hand, leaving the kitchen and passing through the dining room as Danny and Paul end a quick hug, and then Paul sees me.

"Holy shit. Bexley?" He grins from ear to ear. I hurry over to him and hug the boy I've always thought of as a brother but haven't seen since I was thirteen.

"Good God, what have you been up to?" he asks me.

I shrug. "Nothing much. What about you, college boy?" I nudge his shoulder.

He smiles. "I'm going to be mayor of this town one day. Just wait."

"Just don't forget about us little people," I say with a smirk.

"Never," he says. He looks away from me. "Johnny, good to see you."

Johnny nods, shaking his hand. "Yeah, you, too."

"Where's Ma?" Paul questions.

"Kitchen," Danny says. "Johnny is moving out of the foster home, so we'll be out for a bit." He walks past his older brother.

"Be back before dark," Paul says playfully.

Danny grins, his eyes going to me for a quick moment before he exits the house.

Chapter Eleven

Bones
Three days missing

My ribs ache when I breathe, and dried blood is caked on my temple and the side of my face. With the help from the wall behind me, I somehow manage to get back upright in the chair. It's a struggle from hell, especially since I can't use my legs or arms. This motherfucker is making sure I can't get out.

I'm depleted of energy. The only thing keeping me going is the fact she's here with me. And I want to see this man suffer. On top of my exhaustion, I'm troubled that she hates me. And why wouldn't she? I'm not a good man. At one time, I did try to be for her—well, I tried to be around her, but what good did that do? I only got her for a brief moment, and then it was all snatched away.

One minute she was mine, and the next I was on my knees, begging her to change her mind.

But she didn't.

She let me go.

I've felt a knife in my chest ever since. They say young love is fragile, that one wrong move can break it because it's too weak to withstand the hardships of life. But my love for her never faltered even after she chose another man.

And the man she chose.

God.

I never could have imagined her with someone new, but it would have been easier if it were a stranger, or would it? At least I've known she had someone who loved her, who would treat her right, give her the kind of life I couldn't. I realized monsters don't get happily ever afters. It's the good guys who win in the end.

Believe me, though. Time has made me see things that way. I was not so understanding when it happened.

Time has changed a lot. My appearance has grown meaner, rougher. It's transformed who I am on the inside, too. The more days that passed after things went south with us, the more sins I committed.

I put distance between her and me when she made her choice all those years ago. Of course, I still kept an eye on her from afar. I would watch her sometimes, sitting outside the flower shop where she works, but I never went inside.

I let her enjoy her life and I sank deeper into mine. In this type of world, unless you're six feet under, there is no peace. I've done things over these last few years that can't be forgiven.

Genesis

In the back of my mind, I've always known who I am. Known who I wanted to be, and I went after it.

Chapter Twelve
Danny
2003

"He knows you're leaving?" I ask Johnny as we head a few streets over to the place Johnny's been staying since we were thirteen.

"No," he says. "David doesn't even know I'm eighteen now."

I smirk. "This'll be a shock then. One less check he'll be getting a month."

"Yeah," Johnny agrees quietly. "David's sick. I think he messes with the little girls that come through."

"What?" I ask, looking over at him.

Johnny nods with a disgusted look on his face.

I look out the window, my blood turning icy at the thought of a man taking advantage of little girls. Nobody fucks with kids.

"Maybe we should teach him a lesson?" I say, rubbing my chin before taking a sip of my beer.

I look over at Johnny who lifts a brow. "Been wanting to do that," he says. "I've shoved him around a bit, but there's only so much I can do without getting kicked out."

I rest my bottle on my knee. "We'll take him for a walk on the Delaware, yeah?"

Genesis

Johnny licks his bottom lip, twisting his hand around the wheel. At eighteen, Johnny's pretty good at sweeping things up. I'm not the only person watching Moretti and his crew closely. Johnny pays attention to how they don't get caught and he makes sure we do the same.

We pull up to the curb and I look over at the blue house Johnny's been living in.

The sky is as gray as the moon and the leaves tumble on the sidewalk, chasing one another like a cat and mouse. "Pop the trunk," I say as I open the car door. Johnny does and I grab a black hoodie, sliding it over my head. I run my hand through my hair and Johnny shuts his car door.

"He here?" I ask.

Johnny looks toward the side of the house and nods before sliding his hands into his black hoodie.

"Kids should be at school," he says.

"All right," I reply. "Good."

We head up to the front porch. I look in the neighbor's yard, seeing a dog on a thick chain curled up by a doghouse. No car in the driveway. Same with the ones to the left of us.

"What does he like to do?" I ask Johnny.

He lifts his brow.

"I mean, what can we entice him with to get him out of the house?"

My boy nods in understanding. "He likes girls. Let's see if he wants to go to a strip club."

"Think he'll be down for that?"

"He's a fucking pervert, Danny. He'll be down for it." Johnny twists the doorknob and we step inside. The smell of dank weed and booze hits me in the face so hard I have to cover my nose. "Goddamn." I cough. "Smells like a distillery in this place."

Johnny laughs and it's a sound you don't hear too often. "Yo, David," he calls out. We hear grunting and the sound of something breaking. Both of us take off upstairs.

We hit the hall. "It's coming from Carson's room," Johnny says.

I have no idea who Carson is, but when we step into the doorway, I instantly like the boy. He's on top of David, wailing on his face with a gun.

"Jesus," Johnny says, walking over and pulling Carson off the man. But Carson goes back in for another hit, splattering blood on his clothes.

"That's enough," I say.

Carson looks over at me. "Who the fuck are you?"

I lift my chin. "You don't wanna talk to me like that."

Carson smirks, looking back at Johnny. "Who the hell is this guy?"

I step up, quickly grabbing the boy by his throat and shoving him against the wall. I snatch the gun from his hand, putting it against his throat. "I'm

Genesis

Danny. And I'll break every little bone in your face if you disrespect me again."

Carson holds his hands up in surrender.

I let go of his throat. He coughs. "Jesus."

"What happened here?" Johnny asks.

"Motherfucker came in my room without my permission," Carson says, rubbing his neck and giving me a sideways glance.

"So you beat him with a gun?" Johnny asks. "Where did you even get that thing?"

"It pissed me off." Carson shrugs. "And easy—bought it from a guy down the street."

I laugh, looking down at the unconscious man. "Well, we won't have to convince him to leave the house now. Come on, get him up."

I walk into the hall, looking for a bathroom while they pick the man up and haul him downstairs. I grab a towel and wipe my fingerprints from the gun before wrapping it in the towel and following the boys out.

Ice floats in patches on the river as we three stand under the bridge with this sick fuck wrapped in a sheet. I look over at Carson, studying him for a moment. He looks back at me and I narrow my eyes as I hit my cigarette.

"Here," I say, giving him his gun back. He looks a little surprised as he takes the wrapped-up gun, flipping the ends of the towel away from it. David moans from inside the sheet. He starts to move, and before any of us can blink, Carson shoots him three times.

Three times.

Twice in the back and once in the head.

The head would have been enough.

"Jesus. Did you even think about it before you pulled the trigger?" Johnny asks.

Carson laughed. "No."

"Everybody, this is Carson," I say as we walk into the house. Paul and Samuel look our way from watching the football game. They lift their chins in hello to my new friend.

"Food ready?" I ask.

"Almost," Paul says, picking up his beer from the table. I lift my hoodie off and hang it on the coat rack as Carson and Johnny take a seat in the living room. I have other plans, though. I walk past them into the dining room, looking at the table that's already filled with bowls of green beans and sweet potato souffle.

Genesis

"I hope you made some pecan pie," I say, walking into the kitchen.

Ma turns around, grinning at me. "I wouldn't forget your favorite pie."

I give her a kiss on the cheek, seeing there are three pies on the counter. "You made extra?" I ask.

"That's for Mr. Simpson down the street."

"Mr. Simpson?" I ask with a smirk.

"Oh hush," she says, her cheeks turning a shade of pink. She unties her apron. "I'll be right back. I'm going to take this pie to him. Watch the stove for me, please," she says to Bexley. Ma hangs the apron, grabs the pie, and exits the kitchen.

Bexley turns to look at me. "Johnny get moved out okay?"

I scratch the back of my neck. "Yeah. Made a little mess, but we cleaned it all up."

She nods, leaning back against the counter. It's odd seeing her here after all these years. Good, though.

"How have you been?" I ask.

"Great," she says. "You?"

"Good," I reply. I open the fridge and grab another beer, twisting the top off and tossing it into the trash beside her as she crosses her arms. Her eyes move over me before settling on my face.

"Why didn't you visit?" she asks.

"I could ask you the same."

She shrugs with her face. "You stopped coming to my window. I figured you were done with what we had."

"What did we have?" I ask, moving closer to her.

"Secrets," she says, her eyes moving to my lips.

"Secrets," I repeat. "Did you miss me?" I put my beer on the counter.

"Is that what you want to hear?"

I don't answer. Instead, I ask another question. "You and Samuel dating?" I need to know exactly what the deal is here.

She tilts her head slightly. "Are you seeing someone?" she tosses back.

"No one in particular." My eyes bounce down her body.

Her tongue goes to the roof of her mouth as she looks toward the floor. "It could have been you, you know?"

"Me?" I ask.

Bexley looks back at me. "Come on, Danny. You're many things, but you're not stupid. You knew how I felt about you."

"*Felt*? As in past tense?"

"As in time moved on."

I nod and we're interrupted when Samuel walks into the room. He looks between the two of us suspiciously. I grab my beer, and Bexley opens the oven to check the turkey, while I check out her ass.

Genesis

"You coming to watch the game?" Samuel asks, grabbing a soda from the fridge.

"Yeah," I reply. "I was just getting a beer." I make show of it in my hand. He nods, walking over to Bexley.

"Come out here," he says. I watch the two together curiously.

"Be there in a minute. I'm watching this," she nods to the stove, "until Ma gets back."

"Okay. I'll save you a seat." He kisses her forehead, turning around and eyeing me as I chug my beer, trying to cool the fire burning in my chest.

I give him a wink and toss the beer into the trash as he exits the room. I check, making sure he's gone before looking back at her. She licks her bottom lip.

"You're wrong, you know? I never knew how you felt about me because you never said it."

"Yeah, well, neither did you."

"What if I said it now?" I ask, walking closer to her. She swallows as I near. "Would it be too late?"

I'm so close I could kiss her, but I make no move to do so. I reach up and run my finger over the faint scar on her jaw.

Her eyes jump between mine as her pupils dilate. I wonder if she's wet between her legs. God, I'd love to reach my hand down the front of her jeans. I'd love to kiss her throat when her head falls back because I make her feel good.

"Answer me."

"Wouldn't that be breaking the rules or something?" she asks.

"Rules?"

"Ah, come on. You know there was always this invisible line we never crossed."

"What if I crossed it now?"

Her eyes narrow in challenge. "What if you did?"

I bite my lip, looking down at hers.

"Johnny said there was beer in here?" Carson asks, walking in.

I clear my throat and step back from Bexley. Jesus fucking Christ, will these people stay the fuck out? "Yeah, man. In the fridge." I keep my eyes on her as Carson gets what he wants and then leaves the room.

"We're going out after. Come with us," I say.

She makes a face like she's not sure. "I came here with Samuel."

"And you don't want to leave him?" I ask.

"That would be rude, don't you think?"

"I don't care."

"Of course, you don't. But I do."

I nod. "All right. Suit yourself. I better get back out there. He might get suspicious." I smirk and exit the room.

"What do girls and noodles have in common?" I hear Carson say to Johnny as I walk back into the living room.

Genesis

Johnny looks over at him. "The fuck if I know."

"They both wiggle when you eat them," Carson says with a wink.

I grin, taking a seat on the couch. "Where the hell did you get this guy?" Paul asks me.

"Same foster home as Johnny," I reply as Ma walks into the house. I failed to mention that he seems to be a borderline lunatic with psychopathic tendencies, but whatever.

"Turkey's done," Bexley says from the dining room.

"Thank fuck. Let's eat," Paul says, standing up, rubbing his hands together. Samuel stands, too, and Bexley smiles at him as he walks toward her.

"No dirty jokes at the table," I tell Carson.

Like time hasn't passed, we all take our usual seats at the table. Carson pulls up the extra chair that Ma has under the desk by the window.

"I just want to say, I'm thrilled to have all my kids here," Ma says with a smile on her face and a tear in her eye. "Bexley, we missed you."

I look at the girl beside me as she returns Ma's smile.

"I missed you all," she says.

"Yeah, yeah, can we eat already?" Paul says, bringing in the turkey. "Bexley isn't the main show here."

Laughter ignites from the table and Bexley rolls her eyes at my older brother.

"I mean, no offense, Bex, but look at this thing," Paul says, grabbing the knife to cut the turkey.

"None taken," Bexley replies, clearly unoffended because she knows Paul's kidding. "Make sure you don't mess it up with your crappy carving skills," Bexley tosses back. "You remember the last time you got ahold of a turkey."

"Fuck you," Paul says, laughing.

"You boys and your bad language," Ma says.

"Sorry, Ma," Paul replies.

She makes a face like she forgives him, but she still doesn't like it. Samuel leans over to Johnny. "Who put this guy in charge, anyway?"

Johnny grins.

"Finally," I say over to him. "You've had a frown on your face all day."

"You know I save my best smiles for Samuel," Johnny says with a wink.

"What the hell am I, chopped liver? I bring you to dinner and this is how you treat me?" I say, taking mock offense.

Bexley leans over. "Maybe you need a new boyfriend?"

"Maybe I need a girlfriend," I reply.

She smirks but doesn't blush as she looks away.

"What was that?" Samuel asks from the other side.

"Nothing," I say.

Genesis

"Let's bless the food before we all die of hunger," Ma says.

I grab Bexley's hand beside me, and from my peripheral, I see her bow her head. I run my thumb over hers as Ma begins.

"Bless us, O Lord, and these, Thy gifts, which we are about to receive from Thy bounty. Through Christ, our Lord. Amen."

Bexley goes to pull her hand away, but I don't let up. She looks over at me with narrowed eyes as everyone at the table starts passing bowls around, chatting amongst themselves. "Pass me the rolls, would ya?" Samuel says to Bexley. Reluctantly, I let her have her hand back.

Dinner carries on. We joke around, talk about Paul's time in school while Johnny, Carson, and I act like we didn't just kill a man and sink him to the bottom of the river. We eat and share stories, all while Bexley and I pretend like we didn't wish everyone in this room would vanish so we could be alone. Or I wish and like to think she does, too.

Samuel keeps giving me eat shit looks and trying to make a show that he and Bexley might be an item, but she didn't tell me that, so as far as I'm concerned, she's unattached.

Once everyone is done, we clear the table. "Whose turn is it to do the dishes?" Paul asks.

"Danny's," Ma says.

"How the hell is it mine?" I ask her.

"You and Bexley always used to do them at Thanksgiving," she replies.

"Bexley and I can do them," Samuel says.

"Nah. We got it," I reply, picking up his empty plate.

"Go watch the game," Bexley says, giving Samuel a reassuring smile. I smirk as he tries to murder me with his eyes and then I look at Johnny who's watching this whole show with silent curiosity.

I dump the dishes into the sink as Bexley walks in behind me. "What the hell is going on?" she asks. "You never wanted to do the dishes."

"But you're doing them."

"Oh, so all of a sudden you want to?" She turns the water on, filling the sink as I squirt soap in.

"Exactly."

She rolls her eyes. "This is ridiculous."

"What? That I want to catch up with you? I haven't seen you in years, Little Girl."

She gives me the side-eye. "That's your fault."

"It's *our* fault," I reply.

She shrugs, scrubbing a plate and then handing it to me to rinse.

"Tell me about you and Samuel. How did you run into each other again?"

"School."

"Oh, right," I reply, remembering they now attend the same high school.

Genesis

"Why did you drop out?" she asks.

"Had more important things to do."

"Like what I saw earlier?" she asks me with a lifted brow.

"Like, don't worry about it," I reply.

She narrows her eyes at me. "You don't have to live that kind of life, Danny."

"And you don't have to hang out with lame guys like my brother," I reply.

"Samuel isn't lame. He's sweet."

"Sweet?" I ask. "I thought you girls liked the bad boys."

"We like the thought of a bad boy, but it's the sweet ones that win eventually."

I study her for a moment. "I can be sweet," I say.

"You? Sweet?" She laughs.

"What? Why is that so hard to believe? Remember your thirteenth birthday?"

"I remember it very well," she replies. "I remember asking you to stay."

I look down. "It was late. Your mom was a few rooms down."

She frowns. "She was always a few rooms down, Danny."

"Hence the invisible line, huh?" I say.

She doesn't respond, only scrubs another plate a little slower than the other one.

"What are your plans when you graduate?" I ask, changing the subject.

"College," she says.

I nod. "Good."

We make small talk, catching up on everything and learning new things about each other. Of course, I leave out all the details about my "job" and try to keep the subject off me as much as possible. She's right. I don't have to live the life I live, but there's nothing else I'd rather do.

Except maybe be with her.

Chapter Thirteen
Bexley
Three days missing

I can't recall the last time I've been alone with Danny. It's a warm, familiar feeling. It's comfortable even in the worst possible situation. Ever since he asked if I remember the first time we saw each other, I've been thinking about it. I can't help it. What else am I going to do?

My life is in pieces now. I'm stuck God knows where with a man I've trained myself to hate.

Only I *don't* hate him.

I've tried, and I had myself convinced for a long while, but being here now, alone with him, I know I've only been pretending and not just for my sake, but for my husband's as well.

But thinking back on our time spent together only confirms I did the right thing all those years ago, but not before I did the dumbest thing… I still remember the look on his face when I showed up at the clubhouse. And I still remember the feeling I got when he shared one of his biggest secrets with me.

Chapter Fourteen
Bexley
2003

Later, once the kitchen was cleaned and the guys finished the game, everyone went off and did their own thing. Samuel and I decided to watch a movie on the couch after Paul, Danny, Johnny, and that other guy went out. Ma worked on a puzzle until she was too tired to keep her eyes open. She told us goodnight, made me promise to visit, and then went off to bed.

"It's getting late," Samuel says. "You better get back home so your uncle lets you come back."

"Yeah," I reply, looking at the clock and seeing it's almost ten.

Samuel and his caring soul. I really wanted to go out with the boys, but he asked me to watch a movie so…

We stand up and hug. He seems to want to kiss me but makes no move to do so and it reminds me so much of Danny.

He says he's this bad boy, which, come on, he *is*, but I think the brothers have more in common than they think. Except they're also so very different. I kiss him on the cheek. "I had fun. Thanks for inviting me over."

Genesis

"I thought Ma was going to break you, she squeezed you so hard."

I laugh, my eyes looking around the room thoughtfully. "It hasn't changed a bit," I tell him.

"Yeah," he says. "Everyone that's been in it has, though." He looks back at me and I smile wistfully. His eyes shine in the dark-lit room as the low lamp paints the walls gold. Samuel really is the cutest.

"You're sweet, Samuel."

He lifts a brow. "Thanks." He says it like that's not what he wanted to hear.

"There's nothing wrong with that, ya know?"

He nods. "Right."

I grin. "I'll see you at school."

"Be safe," he replies.

Once in my car, I start it, rubbing my hands together to keep warm before I pull my seat belt across me.

I exhale, looking toward the house. Good God, what a Thanksgiving. I smile to myself as I put the car in drive and pull away from the curb, hitting my blinker as I head out of the neighborhood. My mind chases Danny and a thought intertwines. I'm not ready to go home just yet. I remember where Danny took me on my thirteenth birthday, and I decide, even though I know it's not safe, I might swing by there. If I see Danny's car, I'll go in. If I don't, I won't. Simple as that.

Paige P. Horne

Pulling up to the clubhouse where I got my first buzz, I spot Danny's car over on the left side. I open the door, smelling the faint scent of smoke and hearing laughter and music coming from the back. I walk to the door, knocking three times, like I remember Danny doing all those years ago.

A guy with silver hair answers and I remember him.

He narrows his eyes. "You lost?" he asks.

"Um, no, I'm looking for Danny. I'm Bexley, remember? The girl who took all your money in Texas Hold 'em?"

He looks over at me for a moment. "Wait?" he says. "It's you. Damn, you've grown."

I scrunch my nose. "Um, thanks."

"Yo, Danny," he calls out behind him. "Look who came by." He opens the door wider and I see Danny sitting on the couch with a girl in his lap. My heart sinks.

He moves the girl from his lap and takes the smoke from his lips. "What the hell are you doing here?" he asks with a Danny smirk. That's something he's really grown into.

A few people look at me, and I feel my chest turn red.

"Bexley!" I hear someone call out. "Come in," Paul says. "You'll freeze your ass off out there."

Genesis

I look at Danny. "Yeah," he says. "It's fucking cold." He grabs my hand and pulls me inside as he shuts the door. "You remember Mickey."

"She remembers kicking my ass in poker," he replies. "Hey, rematch in a little bit." He points at me.

I smile. "Okay, I'm down to win some money." Mickey laughs and walks to the bar.

"You want a drink or something?" Danny asks me.

"What are you drinking?"

"Nothing. I usually don't around here."

"Why?" I ask.

He winks. "Better that way."

I narrow my eyes in confusion as Paul walks up. "Little Girl is in the clubhouse." He puts his arm around me, pulling me close in a brother-like hug.

"Are you drunk?" I ask him, laughing.

"Not yet, but I will be," he says, letting me go. "And you see that blonde over there?"

I nod, spotting the blonde in a see-through shirt. That's something you don't see every day.

"She's going to be su—"

"All right, man," Danny says, interrupting him. "Why don't you go over and work on that?" He pats his brother's back and gently pushes him toward the woman.

I cover my mouth because I've never seen Paul like this. He's usually the clear-headed one.

"Be safe," he says, turning back and pointing to the two of us. "Love you, Bexley!" he calls out.

I shake my head in embarrassment as Danny laughs, looking down at me. "How about we go somewhere else?"

"You invited me here, remember?" I ask.

"No, I invited you out. Not here."

I look toward the girl who was sitting in his lap. "You don't want me here."

He follows my gaze. "What?" He laughs. "Fuck her. I'd just rather take you somewhere quieter."

I narrow my eyes. "Like where?"

"I know a place," he says.

I look around the clubhouse. It's packed with rough-looking men and women who hardly wear anything. I do feel out of place. It's not exactly as I remember when I was a kid.

"Okay," I say.

He looks surmised. "Wow, she said yes."

I roll my eyes.

"Let's tell Johnny and Paul bye," he says, grabbing my hand again.

After we say bye, we step back out into the cold. "I hope wherever you're taking me, it's warm," I tell him, pulling my coat tighter around me.

"It is," he says. "Come on. Let's take my car."

We head down the road with the heater turned up high. Danny takes us away from the neighborhood and through the shitty town of Postings. Sirens cry

Genesis

in the night and somewhere someone's getting shot or robbed or God knows what.

    I look over at him as we ride in his Impala. He wears jeans and a black hoodie. His knuckles are scarred silver, some with scabs still. His hair is dark and thick, his jawline pronounced. He looks over at me, giving me a curious lift of his lips before going back to the road, but he doesn't say anything as his hand rests lazily on the bottom of the wheel. The radio is a noise filter, high enough to break the silence, yet low enough to help thoughts weave in and out.

    I look out at the lake we now ride beside as the moon shines down on it. What am I doing?

    I'm in the car with Danny O'Brien.

    God, what *am* I doing?

    I'm probably riding with one of the most dangerous guys in Postings, and yet, I've never felt safer. The only thing I've ever witnessed Danny doing was burn down a house, but the stories he told me when we were kids about the men he hung out with. I'm no fool. I know this boy has grown up right alongside them. You pick up things. You adapt to the environment you're around.

    Right now, Danny still has that boyish look, but I know one day, when I look at him, he'll be far from it. He turns and a house comes into view.

    "Where are we?" I ask.

    He puts the car in park. "This is my place."

"What? Your place?" I look back at the house. It's older, needs some work, but it's nice. It's out in the middle of nowhere, surrounded by trees with a lake view. I wonder what it looks like during the day. It's too dark to see every detail.

"How is this yours, Danny?"

"I bought it."

"Well, I get that, but how?"

He bites his inner cheek, moving his eyes away from me. "I have money, Bexley. Lots of it, actually. Hell, I've been making it since I was thirteen and I haven't bought much but clothes and this car."

I narrow my eyes at him. "How do you have money, Danny? You don't even have a job."

"I have a job."

"Where? Where is your job? What do you do?"

"I work for a guy named Moretti."

"And what does this Moretti do?"

"Lots of things," he says.

"Lots of illegal things?"

He shrugs. "What does it matter?"

I scoff. "What does it matter?" I widen my eyes in disbelief. "You could get in trouble. You could get caught and be sent off to prison or something."

"I'm not going to get caught."

"How do you know that?"

"Because I know. In this world, you don't get caught unless you're stupid."

Genesis

"Really?" I ask doubtfully. "And what you're doing isn't stupid?"

"Look, Bexley. This is who I am. This is my life. Is it dangerous?" He lifts his shoulder. "At times, yeah, but you know me. You know I love the thrill. I'm not changing for anyone. You can accept that and we can move forward, or I can take you home right now and you can forget I ever brought you here."

I blink my eyes at him in the low-lit car. There's a security light in the yard and the moon shines brightly through the tree line above us.

"So?" he says. "Which is it?"

"Just like that, I have to choose?"

"Yes," he says.

"Jesus, Danny." I shake my head and take in a breath, rubbing my hand across my forehead. I think about Samuel and how being with him would be so easy. Life would be safe, a little bubble of sweetness. Why am I here? Why did I get in the car with this guy?

You know why, my subconscious speaks up.

I've loved this boy possibly since the first time I saw him. He'd just set a house on fire, and I was amazed. How could two kids do this? And then he followed me when I was running away from the reality of my life. My mom was dying, and I wanted to destroy everything. I recall what he said to me that night.

He looks at me and smiles. "That's always so fun," he says.

"What?" I ask, out of breath.

"Doing something bad and not getting caught," he replies like it's the simplest thing.

I make a face of confusion. "You like doing bad things?"

"Don't you?" he asks. "You were the one busting windows first."

"I was... I wasn't doing it because it was bad. I was doing it because I was mad."

"What's the difference in why? You still knew it was wrong and you still did it. And..." he says all matter-of-factly, "you didn't get caught."

Samuel may be the safe choice, but Samuel isn't making a move. Samuel isn't asking me to choose.

I know this is wrong. I know whatever Danny does isn't good, but there is a part of me that likes that about him. I like the dangerous side.

I look back at him. "Can I see what the inside looks like?"

His lip lifts. He reaches up and removes his keys. "Come on."

He unlocks the door to the cabin in the woods, and we step through. It's warm, so I know he's been here. "I just bought it, so I haven't really done anything to it." He walks over and turns on a lamp before tossing his keys onto the table. He reaches behind his head and pulls his hoodie off, causing his

Genesis

shirt to rise. My eyes jump down to exposed skin, a happy trail that leads to... well, we know where it leads. My body warms, and my heart speeds up.

And things get real.

I'm alone with Danny in *his* house.

He tosses the hoodie onto the back of the couch and I notice a knife hanging on his belt. "Want something to drink?" he asks, running a hand through his hair.

I swallow my nerves.

"No," I say.

He looks over at me. "All right."

"What am I doing here, Danny?" I ask.

"I wanted to show you this," he says, waving his hand around.

I nod, looking around the living room. He lifts his chin, sliding his hands into his pockets. I slide my coat off, tossing it onto the couch beside his. Next goes the long-sleeve shirt I'm wearing over my tank top. He watches curiously and his eyes jump down to my wrist.

"You still wear it?" he asks.

I look down, lifting my arm and running my fingers over the knotted wheat chain. "Why wouldn't I?"

I drop my arm, walking closer until I'm standing right in front of him. I look up, my heart pounding out of my chest. The heat kicks on, swirling warmth through the house, breaking the silence with a low hum. "Guess there's no invisible line here," I say.

He doesn't say anything. I reach up, running my hand under the front of his shirt. Scared, nervous, and every other feeling a person could possibly feel in this moment. He could turn me down. He could tell me to stop. Or he could let me continue and I have no idea what I'm doing.

His skin is warm. He watches me, not moving. I look down at his lips before my eyes bounce back up to his. He tilts his head, looking at my lips, too.

And then I hold on to his belt, lifting my toes so our faces are close.

I lean, he bends, and lightly we kiss. His hands come out of his pockets, gripping onto my hips as my tongue slips past his lips, dancing with his. My hands go to the back of his head and I run my fingers through his hair. Danny's kiss is a mixture of bliss and torture.

I moan into his mouth in pure pleasure. He takes that as permission to keep going, walking us over to the couch. He sits down and pulls me on top of his lap. I adjust my legs, careful of the knife he wears even though it's in a leather holding case. Our lips meet, and our tongues move together. Our make-out session is hot and earth-shattering. He reaches down and pulls my tank top up, breaking our kiss so he can remove it.

Genesis

His face goes to my breast and he kisses the top, licking my skin before pulling the cup down. His mouth goes to my nipple and he sucks and bites gently.

I don't think I've ever been wetter than I am right now. Jesus Christ, I could explode. Quickly, he sits up, moving us on the couch so he is on top. He kisses my stomach before undoing my jeans. I bite my lip as he slides them off of me. Danny runs his eyes up my body, and I feel extremely shy.

"Did you fuck my brother earlier?"

I narrow my eyes. "What? No."

"Why were you upstairs then?" he questions.

"Are you serious right now?"

"Deathly," he says.

"I didn't sleep with Samuel, Danny. I've never slept with anyone."

A crease forms in his brow as he shakes his head. "Wait? What? And you're choosing to sleep with me?"

"Well, I was," I say, rolling my eyes. "But you just fucked that up." I sit up, exhaling as I grab my shirt from the floor.

"Wait," he says. "Shit, I didn't mean to make us stop."

"You just insinuated I was a slut, Danny. You think I'd fuck your brother and then sleep with you on the same day?" I pull my tank top over my head and pick my jeans up, sliding them back up.

"Fuck, Bexley. I'm sorry."

"Wow, Danny O'Brien apologizing. That's something," I say sarcastically. I reach over and grab my long-sleeve button-up from the back of the couch. "Will you take me back to my car?"

He runs his hand down his face. "It's late. Just stay here."

"My uncle will have a fit. I need to get home before he calls the cops."

"Fine," he groans, getting off the couch and grabbing his hoodie. "Let's go."

Chapter Fifteen
Bones
Three days missing

I wiggle my wrists again, wincing. I feel the blood dripping down the palm of my hand from trying to free myself but failing continuously. Through my blindfold, I can see the light again, so I know we've been here for at least three or four days. It's hard to tell, though, and I have no way of knowing how long I was unconscious to begin with.

I have no idea what this guy is planning, but the fact he threatens to take everything from me has me questioning what has already been taken. And I'm afraid Bexley may be right to assume this is all my fault. For some reason, this man wants to ruin me, and she's been caught in the crossfire.

And so has my family.

There's no fucking way this man could know me or else he wouldn't have done this.

I've been rubbing the blindfold against my shoulder and slowly it's starting to loosen. A knife I always carry rests on my hip, covered by my shirt. If I could see better, maybe I could get these zip ties off somehow.

My head still pounds, and sleep wavers on and off. We're both groggy and hungry. The stranger comes back only to feed us, to give us water, and to let us relieve ourselves. The first time he let me loose so I could piss, I made a move. I got some good hits in and almost had him knocked out, until he punched me in the ribs, and I bent over in agony. The second time, he kept a gun pointed at me and has ever since.

He doesn't talk, no matter how hard I try to get him to, and he doesn't linger. My mind is overrun with thoughts of now, thoughts of the past, thoughts of her. I'm one hundred percent sure Moretti has a crew searching for me, and when they find me, whoever this man is, he will die. Because my boys don't play, we have each other's backs and years of trust among the three of us. They will come.

And when they do, God help this motherfucker.

Chapter Sixteen
Danny
2003

"So, what happened between you and Bexley yesterday?" Carson asks from the back seat as we ride through the neighborhood. I look in the rearview.

"Why the fuck is that your business?" I ask.

He holds his hands up. "Hey, just making conversation. Fuck if I care." He looks out the window and I look back in front of me. Johnny doesn't say anything as usual. I haven't talked to Bexley since I dropped her off last night. I told her ass to call me once she got home, but she chose not to. She's pissed at me, and I get it. I basically called her a whore.

I didn't mean to; it just came out wrong. The fact I could have been her first and lost my chance. Let's just say I'm pretty pissed off myself. I just shoved her into my brothers' arms.

I'm a fucking idiot.

Pulling into Moretti's place, I shut the car off and we three hop out.

We walk in the clubhouse and head to his office. "Mickey." I lift my chin at him sitting on the couch before I tap my knuckles against the door.

"Come in," he says from the other side. We walk in and he eyes us. "Why's he here?" Moretti asks, looking at Carson.

"He's with me," I say.

He lifts his brow. "If you say so. Sit down." He points. I walk around and take a seat, as Johnny does the same. Carson sits on the couch.

"What the fuck did you do?" he asks.

I look over at Johnny.

"Don't fucking look at him. Look at me. I got the cops up my ass now. What did you do to him?" he asks, sitting back in his chair.

"Do to who?"

"Don't play dumb, Danny. You know who. Where's David?"

I shrug. "Do you know where David is?" I ask Johnny.

He shakes his head.

"Carson, do you know?"

"Haven't seen him," he says.

Moretti exhales drastically and shakes his head. "Okay," he says. "I see what you're doing here. What'd he do, huh? Slap you around a bit? Told you to piss off one too many times? Huh? Tell me."

"He was fucking little girls," Johnny says.

Moretti lifts a brow, running a hand down his face. "Stupid motherfucker." He grabs a cigar from his box on the desk. "Where is he?" He strikes a match.

Genesis

"River," I say.

"Dead?" he asks, stopping midway from lighting his smoke.

I nod.

"Christ," he says. "So now I have to pay the cops off to fuck around somewhere else. You couldn't have just beaten him? Taught him a lesson?"

"I think we taught him a lesson," I say.

Carson laughs.

Moretti looks at him questionably before focusing back on us. "How about don't kill anybody for a while? I'm deducting this from both of your pay. You'll do some free runs for me."

"Fine," I say.

"Get out of here," he says. "And take that psycho with you."

Carson says, "Hey, I take offense to that."

"You need therapy," Moretti says. "Danny, if he's going to be with you, get his ass some therapy."

"Will do," I reply as we head out the door. We head out to collect Moretti's money from the local business owners, and then we make our way outside of town to grab the new order of moonshine from our guy. By the time we get back, it's getting dark.

"I got something I need to do," I tell the boys when we pull back up to Moretti's.

"Like what?" Johnny asks.

"Like none of your business. I'll see you later."

Johnny gets out and Carson follows, both of them grabbing the crates in the back before I go.

I head to the north side of town, and when I pull up into Bexley's uncle's drive, I get out and walk up to the door. I knock and wait for someone to answer.

Her uncle opens the door. "Bexley here?" I ask him.

He looks down at my clothes and then out at my car. "Who are you?" he asks.

"Danny. Used to live next door before her mom…"

"Oh, the O'Briens," he says. "She's out."

"Out?" I ask.

He nods. "I'll tell her you came by."

"Can I ask who she's out with?"

He narrows his eyes. "I'm sure she'll tell you if she wants you to know."

A car pulls up to the curb, and I turn to look when a woman gets out. "I'll get her to call you," he says, and I take that as my cue to leave.

"Yeah, thanks." I head back to my car, lifting my chin at the woman in hello before I get in. "Where the fuck is she?" I say to myself as I start the car.

I head back to Ma's. I haven't been there all day. Maybe she's there. Last night runs through my mind as I drive on. She's still wearing the bracelet I gifted her on her birthday. I reach for the necklace tucked into my shirt with the knot that matches the

Genesis

one she wears around her wrist as I recall the details of her thirteenth birthday.

Danny
2000

It sits in my pocket as I adjust the ladder so I can climb up into her window. She always leaves it unlocked now. It's our little secret.

I reach the top, seeing her sitting on her bed, watching TV. She looks toward the window and gets up. Walking over, she pushes it up and acts like she's about to help me inside.

"I got it," I say, stepping in.

It's her birthday and she's sitting alone in her bedroom. I don't know why that bothers me.

"Why aren't you out?" I ask her as she sits back on her bed.

She shrugs, gripping the comforter as her hands rest beside her thighs.

I lick my bottom lip, tasting the evening air I've been out in. After I shut the window, I walk over to the chair in the corner of her room, moving clothes to the back of it that she obviously didn't feel like putting up.

I take a seat, exhaling as I look at the TV and running my hands over my jean-covered thighs. She's watching some movie, Pretty Woman, *I think* is the name. I only know because she's watched it before.

"Everything all right?" I ask, not looking away from the TV.

"Yeah," she replies. "What have you been doing all day?"

"You really want to know?"

"Maybe not," she says. She's still dressed in jeans and a tank top.

"Come on," I say, standing up.

"Come on where?"

"It's your fucking birthday, Little Girl. Let's go have some fun."

"I don't know Danny. Mom's really sick tonight."

And that's why she's at home. She's always looking after her mom. I hate that shit. I hate it for her, but mostly, I hate it for me, because when her mom dies, she's leaving.

Part of me wants to stop coming to her room so much, so I can prepare myself for what's to come. I'm a selfish prick. I should be there for her.

"Your mom has her brother if something goes wrong. You only live once. We're going out."

She pulls her bottom lip into her mouth, contemplating what I've said, but she doesn't have a choice. She's coming. "Grab a jacket or whatever. You don't need to wear that tank top."

Genesis

She scoffs. "It's nearly summer. I'm not wearing a jacket, and besides, what's wrong with this?" she asks, looking down at her shirt.

Bexley's thirteen now, and men are perverted assholes, especially some of the ones I know. "Just do what I say," I tell her.

She rolls her eyes. "Fine," she says, standing up. She turns away from me and lifts her shirt up over her head as she walks to her closet. I stare at her back. She has a birthmark near her right hip, and I count the small freckles crawling up her spine. There are four.

She pulls a shirt over her head and turns back around.

"Better?" she asks.

"Better," I reply. "Go tell your mom you're going out with some friends."

"Okay," she says. "Be back."

I sit in her room as she goes and talks to her mom. I've been in here several times since she moved next door. Her mom is getting sicker by the day, and Bexley is a sad person. She doesn't talk about it, but it's the elephant in the room.

I look at the white comforter with colorful flowers on it. My eyes roam over the CDs she has near her stereo and the posters she has up of boy bands. Candles sit on her dresser, and on her nightstand rests a small picture frame of her and her mom. She walks back into the room.

"*She's asleep, so I left a note.*"
"*Okay.*"

We both climb down the ladder, and I move it out of sight as we take off down the street. Johnny will have something to say about this, but I don't give a shit. Tonight, I'm hanging with my girl, because she isn't like other girls.

Bexley is cool. She may be younger than me and the girls I mess around with, but she's older in the way she acts and carries herself. She's not immature and doesn't laugh when something is not funny. She doesn't get mad for no reason, and she doesn't play games.

Bexley's straight-up.

"*Where are we going?*" *she asks.*

"*I want to take you to where I hang out.*"

She looks over at me. "*Danny, I don't think that's a good idea.*"

"*Bexley, it's fine. These people are like family, just like you.*" *I feel her looking at me, so I turn to look at her.*

"*My family's dying,*" *she says, and even as she says it, she shows no emotion. She sheds no tears, but it breaks my cold heart.*

I don't respond, and we keep walking until we reach Moretti's place. It's a hole-in-the-wall spot, where he has poker games and guys come and hang out. His office is here, and in the back are a courtyard with iron back chairs and a fire pit.

Genesis

Nothing fancy, but everyone needs to have a first drink at some point, and I figured why not let Bexley have her first with me.

We walk through the door and a few of the men call out. "Danny boy." I nod and take her hand. "Is this your girlfriend, Danny?" Mickey asks.

"This is Bexley," I reply, seeing Johnny sitting on a couch near the back. He's looking at us, so I lift my chin at him.

"Good to meet you, Bexley. Any friend of Danny's is a friend of ours."

"It's her birthday," I tell him. "We got anything, like a cake or something?"

"We can get one. I'll get one of the boys to run up the street."

"You don't need to do that," Bexley says.

"It's your birthday. You're gonna have cake," I tell her. I walk over to a cooler and grab a beer. "Here. Have a fucking drink and stop being so damn sad."

"I'm not sad," she says, taking the beer from my hand.

"You're lying," I reply, taking the beer back so I can open it for her. She doesn't say anything as I give it back.

"The taste isn't that great at first, but you'll get used to it."

We walk over to the couch and take a seat with Johnny.

"Hey, Johnny," she says.

He nods, looking at me.

"It's her birthday, Johnny. Tell her happy birthday."

"Happy Birthday, Bexley," he says, unenthused.

"Thanks," she mutters as she picks at the label on the beer. We three sit on the couch and watch the guys play poker.

"I'd like to play," Bexley says.

"You wanna play poker?" I question.

"Yeah," she says.

"All right," I reply. "Come on, Johnny. You're playing, too."

That evening was one of the best and worst I've ever had. Turns out, Bexley is one hell of a poker player. Apparently, her uncle taught her. She's got one of the greatest poker faces around. She took all their money. A boy called Beefy, because he has fat fingers, brought in the cake and the whole place went crazy.

"Happy Birthday to you! Happy Birthday to you! Happy Birthday, dear Bexley. Happy fucking Birthday to you!"

"Now give us our money back!" one of the guys yells. Bexley laughs, looking tipsy from the three beers she's consumed. "Winning is winning," she says. "Not my fault you suck."

Genesis

My eyes widen a tad, because if a man would have said that to these guys, they'd get their face slapped. But they shock me stupid and shrug, like she's just telling the truth. I sit on the couch with Johnny as she plays another round. Johnny takes a sip of his beer. "What are you doing?" *he asks me.*

"What are you talking about? I'm sitting here with you."

"No, I mean with Bex."

"It's her birthday, Johnny. The girl was sitting at home by herself with her dying mom."

"And you know this because?"

"Because none of your business."

He looks over at me, narrowing his eyes. "You shouldn't have brought her here."

"Why the fuck does it matter to you?" *I ask.* "Why the fuck do you care if she's sitting at home on her birthday?"

"You don't care about Bexley at all?" *I question.* "She's kept one of our biggest secrets, Johnny. She can be trusted."

"She's a distraction for you."

"Distraction from what?"

"The life we're going to have. She doesn't fit into this world."

I look at her playing poker with the guys. She's put her brunette hair up and she's makeup-free. She laughs when a guy folds and she shows her cards. And like a punch to the gut, I really see her for the first time. She's not just pretty. Bexley's beautiful. Normally, she doesn't smile a lot, and she never looks carefree, but right now she does. Tonight, she looks like a weight has been lifted and for once she isn't thinking about what her future holds.

However, I also see something else. I see the harsh truth of the situation. Bexley is playing poker with a bunch of first-degree murderers. She's taking money from men who don't regret the bad shit they've done.

And after this is over, she'll still go home to a mother who's dying. She's still going to leave.

And she needs to. Bexley is too good for this neighborhood and the monsters living in it. Including me.

Johnny's right. She doesn't fit into the lifestyle we want to live. She may be having fun now, but if she knew what these men did, she wouldn't be cool with it. She would probably be horrified and would run far away from here.

"You're right," I tell him. "She shouldn't be here."

I see the game is over, so I stand up. Walking over to the table, I lean down. "We need to go. It's getting late."

"Aw, one more round," Nugget says.

"Nah," I say. "We need to go."

He stands up, a little drunk from the way he's swaying. "I said one more round, you little shit."

Genesis

I feel my jaw tighten. I can't stand this motherfucker and I don't trust him.

I'm only fifteen but, I swear to God, if he comes around this table, I'll break a chair over his face.

"And I said, it's time for us to go."

He points at me. "You got a bad attitude, little kid."

"Don't call me that," I say with a deadly smirk.

He laughs. "Or you'll what?"

Without a second thought, I lift the chair and throw it at him across the table. Before he can react, I round the table. Picking up the chair, I shove it into his ribcage, causing his drunk ass to hit the floor on his knees. I grip the chair, hitting my foot against the leg of it. Snapping it off, I whack him on the head like I'm Derek Jeter hitting the lead-off home run in game four of the World Series. Blood splatters from his face, and the crowd goes wild, extremely satisfying me. I hit him repeatedly, over and over until his face is nothing but...

"That's enough," Moretti says from the chair he's occupying.

I snap out of my daydream as I grip the chair Bexley sits in.

"Better listen to your boss," I say to Nugget. "Come on, Bexley." *I stand by her seat, waiting for her to get up.*

She does and I take her hand, looking at Nugget one more time before we turn to leave. I look over at Johnny as we walk out the door. He stares at Nugget, clearly watching my back.

"What the hell was that?" Bexley says once we're on the street.

"Nothing," I reply.

She laughs. "That obviously wasn't nothing."

She trips over her feet. "Whoa," I say. "Are you drunk?"

She giggles. "You think?"

I smile at her, amused by her state. She's had several beers and she's tiny. "I'd be impressed if you weren't. Come on, drunk girl. Let's get you home."

Once we climb into her room, I shut the window and watch as she lies down on her bed.

I remember the bracelet in my pocket. Her eyes are shut, and for some reason, I get really nervous. "Hey, Little Girl, wake up," I say, sitting down at the end of her bed. She opens her eyes.

"I'm awake."

"I got you something," I tell her.

She smiles and sits up. "What?" she asks excitedly.

I scoff. "It's not a new car or anything." I reach into my pocket and pull out the silver bracelet. It has a knot on it. I don't know why I got it.

Yeah, I do.

It means something to me because I have a leather necklace that has one, too, but I'm not going

Genesis

to tell her that, and she can't see it because it's in my shirt. This will connect us always. I don't know shit about love or anything, and I have no vision for our future together.

Hell, if anything the girl should stay away from me. So, no matter where she is in life, no matter what happens after her mom dies, my necklace and her bracelet will tie us together.

She looks at the sliver wheat chain in my hand, and her eyes jump back to mine as I study her expression cautiously. I've never given a girl anything, and now I've given the most important one in my life a gift that means never forgetting.

I hope that every time she looks at this, she will think of me. Of course, I'd never tell her that shit.

"Happy Birthday, Bexley," *I say, trying to make like this isn't a big deal.*

She plucks the bracelet from my hand and runs her thumb over the knot.

"Why the knot?" *she asks, tilting her head to look at me, and, of course, she would. Why can't she be like other dumb girls and not question everything?*

I shrug. "Thought it was different."

She narrows her eyes slightly, not believing me, but she lets it go.

"Will you put it on me?" *she asks.*

I reach over and grab it as she flips her small wrist over. I gently touch her soft skin as I link the chain.

She spins it, feathering her digits over the silver, smiling a little. "Thank you," she says. "I'll cherish it forever."

I swallow the feelings I have for her. "Cool," I reply. "Well, I better go."

"Go?" she asks. "Don't you want to watch a movie or something?"

"It's late and you're drunkish."

"Ish," she says with a smile. "Come on. Stay."

I do think about it, and that's what makes me say no. "I'll see you tomorrow. Get some sleep, birthday girl."

She nods. "Okay."

Chapter Seventeen

Bexley
Five days missing

The wind howls outside the windows, and every now and again I can feel a mouse run across my shoe. The first time made me scream, and I nearly flipped over, but thankfully, I caught myself. The thought of my face being on that floor scares me more than the darkness surrounding us.

Danny and I make small talk, and he tries to make me laugh, which is odd. He never was a big jokester, well, not really. There was a time or two he was pretty clever, even if his puns weren't a laughing matter. Danny always made light of the shit he did. He acted as if his *job* was just as normal as a man going to clock in at the factory or something.

I don't think he ever fully understood how much it bothered me. How heavy it weighed on my chest—that the man I loved was a criminal.

"Got it," he says.

"Got what?" I ask, looking around and seeing nothing but this damn blindfold.

"My blindfold."

"Oh good! Can you see where we are? Good God, I'm so glad one of us can actually fucking see. How did you get the thing loose with no…?"

"Holy fuck," he says on a whisper.

"What?" I ask, panicky at the seriousness of his tone. "Danny, what is it?"

"We look like shit," he says playfully, but I can still hear that hint of worry in his voice.

"Really?" I scoff. "I thought I'd look good after being kidnapped, drugged, starved, and tied to a chair for days."

"Yeah, well, you look worse than me," he says.

I roll my eyes, hoping that's not true, but also hoping it is. I worry about his injuries. I can't see them, and it's driving me insane. Shit, even if I could, there isn't a damn thing I could do. I'm no doctor, and I'm sure wherever we are doesn't have a first-aid kit.

"Where are we?" I ask.

"A cabin. It's old. And from the looks of it, it seems like we're way the hell out here."

"Out where?" I ask.

"I have no idea, Bexley. I was just as unconscious as you were when we arrived."

"Don't be a smartass, Danny. I just want answers. I'm the one who still can't see."
A truck pulls up in the front. "Oh, shit. What will he do knowing your blindfold is off?"

"We'll have to see, won't we?"

Genesis

Terror fills my veins, sending my heart nearly into cardiac arrest. I can't imagine being out here without him. His attitude could get him killed.

"Danny, please don't instigate anything with him. Please."

"Don't worry, Little Girl. I won't leave you."

I don't reply as the door opens and I hear boots.

"Now I get to see what all the fuss is about," Danny says.

Fuck.

The man laughs. "You think I care? I knew you'd get that damn thing off eventually, and that's exactly why I'm wearing a mask."

"You're wearing a mask because you're a fucking coward." I hear Danny spit on the floor.

"Careful. You don't know who you're talking to."

"Show me then. Show me who I'm talking to. I'd like to get a real good look at you before my boys come and cut your fucking body parts off and feed them to you."

"Your boys ain't coming anywhere near here. Trust me." I hear the man walk closer to me and I lean back, my hands shaking from nerves. He yanks the blindfold off my face.

"You might as well be able to see, too. I'd hate for you to die blind."

I wince from the harsh light pouring into the room. The urge to rub my eyes is nearly overwhelming and I wiggle my hands in protest.

"God, why won't you let us go, you psychotic motherfucker?" The force of his hand against my cheek nearly knocks me out.

"No!" Danny yells. "Don't you fucking touch her." I hear Danny's chair move and then fall over. He grunts in pain.

"Shut up," the man says. My ear rings a steady low tune. My jaw throbs and my skin burns. I blink my eyes, trying to get ahold of myself. Jesus Christ, I've never been hit so hard in my life. I lick the side of my lip, tasting copper and wincing from the cut that's now there. His hand covered the whole side of my face.

"I'm trying to calm shit down out there. Ya know, the whole search party bullshit." He walks over to Danny and lifts him back upright. "And when I do, I'll be bringing you things that only your loved ones valued. They'll be newspaper clippings of a tragic murder that happened to a sweet old lady. She did live in a bad town, after all.

"And then you'll read in the headlines." He waves his hand in the air dramatically. "A ruthless politician was sleeping with his family close by, tucked safely in their beds when his throat was slit on a Sunday morning."

Genesis

"No one gives a fuck about a dirty politician anyway. Oh, wait. You do," he says to Danny.

I look over at Danny. His jaw is tight, and I'm shocked it doesn't snap at the way this man is talking about killing his family.

My family.

He wears a black ski mask, and he's about six-two I'd imagine. He's got to weigh over two hundred pounds, and most of that seems to be muscle, except for his belly, which pokes out just enough for you to know it's there.

"Curse a God on you altogether. You will suffer for this. Mark me," Danny says so eerily it sends chills down my own spine.

The man laughs. "Oh, Bones, you and your Irish curses. Your father was a fool, and so are you. You can't outlive the kind of life you've chosen, and you won't."

Danny looks to the floor, and I swallow. I've never seen him so helpless, and because I know he doesn't want me to, I look away.

Chapter Eighteen
Bexley
2003

I hop out of my car, my hands full of books from my study session with a group from school. Walking into the house, I hear Hale and a woman laughing.

"Hey," I say, kicking the door shut behind me.

"In here," Hale says. I drop the books onto the key table and walk into the living room.

"Bexley, this is Trinity. She'll be having dinner with us."

"Nice to meet you," I say with a smile.

"And you," she says. "I hope you like breakfast. It's the only thing I can cook, and your uncle here is making me show off my mediocre skills."

I laugh. "It's the most important meal. I'm good with breakfast."

"Great." She smiles.

"Hey, a guy came by here looking for you."

"A guy?" I ask.

"Yeah. Danny was his name."

"Oh," I say, looking for the cordless phone.

"Oh?" he repeats. "You don't sound too enthused."

Genesis

"Kinda mad at him right now," I say, spotting the phone by the candy dish on the bar.

"Do I need to kick his ass?" Hale says.

I laugh. "Nope. Thanks, though." I grab the phone and run up to my room, shutting the door behind me. I dial the O'Briens' number, and then I freak out that Samuel might answer so I hang up.

Crap. I can't ask for Danny if Samuel answers.

I sit down on my bed, looking at my reflection in my vanity mirror. What the heck am I going to do here? I bite my lip, lifting my hair from my neck. If Samuel answers, then I'll just talk to him. If Ma answers, then I'll ask for Danny, and if Danny answers, then great.

I roll my eyes at how ridiculous this is. I should tell Danny to fuck off and forget about it all. But like an idiot, I dial the number again. It rings three times, and then a voice sounds on the end. I exhale in relief.

"Hey," I say.

"Where have you been?" he asks.

"Out," I reply. "You came all the way to my house?"

"Yeah. You didn't call me last night. You could have been dead somewhere."

I smile at myself in the mirror. "You were worried?"

"Shut up," he says. "Let me come get you."

"Fine," I reply. "Come get me."

Paige P. Horne

The movie theater shouldn't be a place to get physical, but somehow, I find my lips on Danny's again. We sit at the top in the very back corner. There's hardly anyone in here, and I'm dying to leave.

"Let's go back to your place," I say.

I know his answer before he even speaks.

"Why not?" I ask.

"I don't want your uncle to get the wrong idea," he says.

"Huh?"

"I picked you up, Bexley. I can't bring you home late."

"You're kidding me, right?"

"No. You didn't see the way he looked at me earlier."

"I didn't think you gave a shit what people thought of you."

"When it comes to you, I do."

I scan his face, my eyes blinking.

"I care about you, Bexley. I don't care about shit else, but when it comes to you, I fucking care. I don't want your uncle keeping you from me. It won't be good for any of us."

Genesis

I sit back, exhaling my disappointment.

He grabs my hand, bringing it to his lips. "Come on," he says, standing up.

I have no idea what we're doing, but something tells me I'd follow this boy into the pits of Hell and smile about it. We exit the theater, and Danny starts his car once we get in. He drives down the road until we're close to the neighborhood. Pulling over between two cars, he shuts the lights off and looks over at me.

"Get in the back," he says.

"What?" I ask with a curious smirk. He opens his car door.

"You heard me," he says.

I reach and climb over the seat into the roomy back, looking out the tinted window before he opens the door and gets in. He shuts it, and in one swift move, he grabs the back of my neck and kisses me crazy. I moan, loving the way his tongue feels like silk heaven.

"Do you like the fact a person like me who does really bad things only cares about you?" he asks, reaching his hand down to my jeans.

"Yes," I say without thought, because I do.

I *really* do. It turns me on. When a bad boy like Danny doesn't give a fuck about anything, but then wants to impress my uncle for me… well, screw me sideways.

"You may act like an angel, but I know the real you, Bexley. I know you like the bad, just like I do."

My button snaps free. My zipper is pulled down.

"Do you know how often I've thought about this?" he asks.

"If it's as much as me, then I won't feel as dirty," I say with a smirk as he pulls my pants down.

He laughs. A sweet, deep sound comes from his chest. "I'm not fucking you in this car. I care about you too much for that, but I am going to make you come."

I can't talk. He's taken the sound from my voice. With hands that have done more violence than I'll probably ever witness, he pulls my baby blue lace panties down my thighs. "Anybody ever touched you like this?"

I find my voice. "You know the answer to that," I reply.

He smirks and I die. His fingers slide over me with easiness.

"Jesus," he says, his voice husky. I should be embarrassed, but I'm not. I don't give a shit. I might be if it was a different boy, but it isn't.

Danny slides a finger inside me. It's odd, but a good odd. He dips another in, and I wince.

"All right?" he asks.

Genesis

I nod as he moves his fingers. There's no way in hell I'm going to have an orgasm, but I'll let him try.

I watch his face as he looks down at me, the concentration, the pouty lips. In this moment, I realize I might be in love with this boy. My heart slows, my mind calms, and I just feel. He keeps going, and I let my head fall back, my eyes shut, and I feel a warmth flow through my chest. I snap my eyes open when someone taps on the window.

Danny stops. "Shit," he says, annoyed.

"Who's in there?" the cop questions.

"Oh my God," I say, covering my mouth as embarrassment floods me.

"Put your clothes on," he says to me.

"My uncle is going to murder me." I quickly grab my panties and slide them on before grabbing my jeans.

"He's not going to murder you." Danny laughs, and I don't know what the hell is so funny.

"Let the fucking window down," the cop says.

"You good?" he asks me.

"Yes," I reply, feeling the burn in my cheeks.

Danny opens the car door. "Officer Radcliff," he greets, stepping out.

"Oh, fucking hell. Danny O'Brien."

Danny shuts the door behind him. I watch through the tinted window, trying to listen.

"What the hell are you doing in the back seat of the car, parked on the side of the road?" he asks.

"Now that would be none of your concern," Danny replies, coolly sliding his hands into his hoodie.

"Who you got in there? A whore? I could lock you up for that, you know?"

"Don't be bitter 'cause the wifey ain't giving you none back home."

"Watch it, Danny." The cop points at him. "By the way, Warren Callie sends his regards. Says he doesn't appreciate you beating up on his men outside of convenience stores."

"Fuck him and you, crooked ass pig."

"You fucking sorry thug. Get the hell off my streets."

Danny laughs. "I think you know these ain't your streets." He yanks open the driver door and gets inside. The cop steps back, mean mugging Danny. Danny puts the car in drive and steps on the gas.

"Fucking pigs," he mutters.

"Danny, what the hell just happened?" I say from the back seat. He looks in the rearview mirror. "Come up here."

I reach up and climb over the seat. "How can you talk to a cop like that?"

"He isn't a good guy, Bexley."

"And you are?" I ask. "Who's Warren?"

Genesis

He exhales. "Don't worry about it."

"I am worried about it. We were just... well, you know what we were doing."

"What were we doing?" he interrupts me, smirking.

"Stop," I say. "This is serious."

He rolls his eyes. "It's not serious. It's just another dirty cop. Forget about it."

But I can't forget about it. How deep is he into this world? This is scary stuff. I look out the window as we head back to my house, picking at the skin on the side of my thumb. I don't really know what to think about all of this.

Danny told me who he was, and like a naïve girl standing on the inside of her front door, I invited the vampire in, and now what's done is done.

"Look, I'm sorry you had to see that," he says. "But you're not stupid, Bexley. You know the world can be a cruel place. Most people just don't see it, is all."

"Yeah," I agree. "Most people don't."

He grips the top of the wheel, resting back in the seat as we drive, and before long we're pulling up in my driveway.

"I'll walk you up," he says, putting the car in park.

"That's okay," I say. "I'll call you tomorrow."

He frowns. "We okay?"

"Yeah," I reply. I lean over and give him a kiss. "Be safe."

"Okay," he says.

I walk across the yard, stepping onto the sidewalk that leads to the door, feeling his eyes on me the entire time. I give him a wave and step inside, shutting the door. I peek out the window, seeing him reverse the car, and I watch until his taillights are out of view.

Part of me is terrified that I'm hanging around someone like him. But the other part understands what Danny is saying. The world is a cruel place. It took my mom when I was just a kid. There's evil no matter where you go, but there's also good, and I'm sad to say that I don't think Danny sees any of the good.

"Are you home?" I hear from the living room. I move away from the small window beside the door and walk in.

"Hey, sorry about skipping out on supper with you and Trinity."

"It's fine," Hale says. "I get you're young. I'm not that old, ya know?"

I smirk. "I didn't say you were." Truthfully, Uncle Hale is only a handful of years older than me. He was my mom's younger brother. The only family member I have left.

"You like this boy?" he asks.

"Something like that."

Genesis

"Something like that?" he questions.

"It's complicated."

"Oh," he says. "He looks a little rough around the edges."

"He's a good guy," I say, defending Danny even though I know Hale is right. Danny looks just like he is: trouble.

And I just lied to my uncle because I'm not so sure Danny is a good guy.

"If you say so," he says. "Wanna play Texas Hold 'em?"

"I'll pop some popcorn," I say.

Chapter Nineteen
Bones
Five days missing

After the man leaves, I look over at Bexley. Her face is starting to swell, her lip is bleeding, and I just sat here and let that happen to her. I sat here and let him talk about my family the way he did, and the worst part of it all? We had to let him feed us because God only knew how long before we'd get to eat again.

Swallowing one's pride is one thing, but this... this is beyond.

"I'm sorry," I say.

"For what?" she asks, her eyes sparkling with tears she didn't want to shed in front of him.

"For being worthless. I didn't do anything. I didn't..."

"Danny, you couldn't have. Your legs and arms are tied. I should have kept my mouth shut. This is not your fault." Tears run down her face, mixing with blood. "God, look at you."

I was only joking when I told her she looked bad because I know I look worse. I'm bloody and bruised. I probably look horrifying to her.

"What did he do to you? Why is this happening?" She looks down, her shoulders trembling as she cries. "Why has my whole fucking life been a shit show?" She kicks her feet, hitting the bottom of the chair continuously. "Goddammit motherfucking shit!" she cries and kicks and... *crack*. The chair snaps from under her and she crashes to the ground.

"Bexley!" I say.

She's tipped over, her head against the wall, and then all of a sudden, she starts...

"Are you laughing?" I ask, confusion taking first place in all the emotions I feel.

She rolls her forehead against the wall, her body shaking as she laughs uncontrollably.

I smirk, but then she looks at me. She sniffs and says, "A person should laugh before they die."

And none of this is funny.

Chapter Twenty
Danny
2003

A few days later, the cops questioned Carson and Johnny about David's strange disappearance. They lied. Johnny said he had no idea where the man went. He'd moved out already. Carson said he was staying at Johnny's, so he didn't know either. They asked if either one of them had an alibi and, of course, that was me.

The cops didn't believe either one of them, though, and said it was too coincidental. So what happened? Like Moretti said he would—he paid them off and told them to fuck around somewhere else.

And that's exactly what they did.

It was all too easy.

And it was another learning experience. Money talks to even the best of men.

Thanksgiving was nearly a month ago now, and Bexley and I have seen each other almost every day since. I take her to the movies, where she ends up all over me and I have to reluctantly take her back home with blue balls so her uncle doesn't stop her from seeing me. I've been jacking off so much lately, it's starting to become a habit.

Genesis

She has no idea what she does to me. I know this world is fucked up, but being with her makes me wonder if maybe there's still some good in it. If maybe one day we could live a good life together. I could save up all the money I make and take her away from here, but then I wonder if it would satisfy me.

To live a clean life—I'm just not sure, and right now, I don't think I have to be. We're young as fuck. Who knows what the future holds? I'm happy to be around her a few hours a day, and the other few I do shit that makes my black heart sing.

Like hit people in the face if they don't pay. "I'll have the money next week," Mr. Walsh says to Johnny.

"Not gonna work," Johnny replies.

"Moretti needs it now," Carson says. "Or we can't promise Warren's men aren't going to come by tonight and rip this whole place apart."

"Please, Danny." The older man looks at me. I've known him since I was a boy playing stickball in the streets. I think I actually busted his window one time. Ma gets her handmade quilts washed here.

I tilt my head. "Sorry, Mr. Walsh. It's a dog-eat-dog world. Gotta pay up. You know that's the way this works."

The man starts cussing us in Italian, waving his hands in the air. He can be dramatic all he wants, but he better hand me the fucking money.

Moments later, I'm lighting a smoke as I head out of the Laundromat. "Gotta go," I say to Johnny.

"Yeah, yeah," he says as he and Carson walk past the car. I reach to open the door as an all red Cadillac rides by and three men stick their heads out.

"Get the fuck down," I yell as the guys in the car fire their guns at us. Glass shatters as we cover our heads, bullets flying past us, hitting the car and making it bounce. Carson stands up and fires his gun after them, but they speed off.

"It's fucking Warren's men," he says.

I wipe the glass from my sleeves. "Christ, look at my car." I lift my hands like *what the hell?* Sirens ring in the distance. "Goddammit. Let's go," I say. I open the door and get in.

"There's glass everywhere," Carson says.

"Wipe the seat with your jacket and come on." I start the ignition, and as soon as Carson shuts the door, I speed off toward Moretti's. I gotta hide this car.

"I'm getting my ass cut to pieces back here," Carson complains.

"Where's your car?" Bexley asks as we walk out to the truck I borrowed from Mickey.

Genesis

"In the shop."

"Oh," she says. I open the truck door for her to climb in. I can't help it, I smack her ass when she does. She looks back at me and smiles. "I hope my uncle didn't see that."

I turn to look at the house. "I hope he didn't either." We head down the road, and I put my arm across the bench seat.

"Where are we going?" she asks.

"I dunno? Want to see a movie?"

"We've seen every movie there is right now."

"True," I say. "You hungry?"

"No."

"There's a concert going on downtown. Wanna see that?"

"No."

I look over at her. "What do you wanna do?"

She shrugs. "Let's go back to your house."

I lift a brow at her. "All right," I say with a nod.

We haven't been back to my place since I accused her of sleeping with my brother. I wonder how things are going with her and him at school, but I don't ask either of them. She hasn't mentioned it, and I don't think it's a good idea for me to bring it up.

The drive is quiet. Me in my own thoughts about Warren and his fucking bitch ass men who shot up my car. If he would stay off of Moretti's turf, we wouldn't be having an issue, period. Why can't people just do what they're told?

Retaliation will have to be asserted. Those fuckers ain't getting away with that shit. I remove my arm from around Bexley and grab my smokes from the dash, rolling the do-it-yourself window down a tad so I don't smoke her out. I pull one out with my teeth and toss the pack back. Lighting it, I exhale stress and rest my hand at the bottom of the wheel.

Mickey makes good money; I have no idea why he drives this old thing. He's Moretti's right-hand man, for fuck's sake. But then again, I think he might be like me. I like nice clothes and shit, but I'm not flashy. I don't have to have the best of the best. I just need to get by.

I hit my smoke, leaving it between my lips as I adjust the heat so she's not cold. It's still early. The sun has just started to set, painting the sky in tangerine orange. The cold wind wisps by the window, and headlights fly by us. I hit my blinker and turn down the long drive that's parallel to the lake.

Bexley looks out at it. She's also quiet. I wonder what she's thinking. Definitely not the same shit I am.

Hell, she's still in school. We have totally different lives. Johnny's words flow through my mind.

Genesis

"She doesn't fit into this world."

She may not fit into the world we're a part of, but she fits in with *me* just fine.

I pull up to the house and kill the engine, letting up the window. I open the door and step out, waiting for her to do the same. She puts her hands in her coat's pockets and I hit my smoke one more time before tossing it into the yard, blowing away from her. I grab the key from under the dead plant on the porch and open the door.

We walk inside, and I lift my hoodie off, throwing it on the sofa. She removes her coat and pulls her sleeves over her palms. "You all right?" I ask.

"Fine," she says, giving me a small smile.

I walk over and adjust the heat because it's fucking cold tonight. Out the living room windows a flock of birds fly across the lake, and the setting sun paints the water red-orange. I bought a small radio, so after I turn the heat up, I flip it on, hearing Coldplay sing about nobody saying it was easy.

Bexley looks out the windows, watching the sun fall. I stand by the couch, looking at her with her arms crossed, her hip to one side, her hair falling down her back.

"Hey, Little Girl, come here."

She turns to look at me, biting her smile. She drops her arms and walks over to me. I look down at her pretty face.

Paige P. Horne

I look at her. *Really* look at her. Her hazel eyes, her hair, her lips. I wish I knew what the future held for us; I wish I knew that what we have right this very moment would never fade.

"What is it?" she asks, looking concerned.

"Will you be my girlfriend?" I ask lowly.

She smiles. "Yeah."

Neither of us goes on about it. Instead, I kiss her. Slow at first, and then the fire builds like it always does, except this time, we're here, alone in my home. A home I hardly come to. A place I just bought. She's the only other person who's been here besides me. I may give her a key, just so she can always have a place to come when she wants to get away, but I'll think about that later.

Right now, I want to show her how I feel. I reach down and grab her thighs, lifting her.

"Wrap your legs around me," I say. I walk down the hall toward the back bedroom as she kisses my neck, running her fingers through my hair.

I lay her down, kiss the scar on her jaw, and reach down to undo her jeans. She watches me as I untie her shoes. She kicks them off and helps pull her pants down. Sitting up, she removes her shirt and unclasps her bra. I look down at her, mesmerized.

This isn't my first time. Hell, I lost that when I was fifteen. There're always easy women around the clubhouse who will do anything for money. One

Genesis

night, Moretti hired a bunch of hookers and Johnny and I had a good time, except they didn't think we were as young as we were.

But this is my first time doing this with someone I care about.

This is Bexley Walker.

Her laugh alone turns me on because it's authentic and raw. I grab her ankles and pull her down the bed closer to me. A laugh escapes her, and she looks up at me. Her hands reach for my belt, and I let her undo it, along with my button and zipper. She lifts my shirt and kisses my stomach.

I grab her hair, twisting it around my fist, angling her head so I can kiss her. I take my knife off my belt, tossing it onto the floor before she slides my jeans down and I step out of them. I climb on top of her as she lies back.

I spread her legs with my body, feeling her hands go up the back of my shirt as she brings it over my head. I drop it on the floor after I pull it off and look down at her. "Oh my God," she whispers, running her fingers over the necklace I wear.

My arms shake as I hold myself up, watching the emotion sweep over her face. That look just killed me. Left me dead. She just stole my heart.

Her eyes go to mine. "I love you," she says.

My lips lift, and I kiss her, swallowing her words so she can't ever have them back. She grabs my face, and I reach down and grab the hem of her panties, slipping them off. I dip my fingers inside of her, happy that she's turned on. This will make it easier on her.

I don't ask permission. I don't ask her if she's ready because there's no going back now. It's too late for mind changing. I push her thighs wider apart and slide inside slowly. She sucks in a harsh breath, and then I go all the way in. I kiss her neck and chest, not moving.

"Breathe, love," I say. She exhales, and I move my hips. Her nails scratch my back, her eyes shut, and I drive on. I feel it when she relaxes, and I capture her little moans, kissing her lips and biting her tongue. She feels amazing. I want her to enjoy this. I want her to always remember it. I reach down and rub her clit. Her mouth falls open as a rush of air releases from her lungs. I bend my elbow, holding on to the side of her head, gripping her hair between my fingers. She hooks her arms around my neck.

Her thighs shake around my waist, and the veins in her neck protrude as she shuts her eyes, bucking beneath me, her feet dinging into the comforter. I don't stop the momentum. I don't go faster. I just let her feel. She opens her eyes, and I can't help the smirk that spreads across my face.

"Feel good?" I ask, panting.

Genesis

"You know it did." She kisses me, and I chase my release. Resting both elbows on the bed, I drive forward until my thighs burn and she milks me dry.

Out of breath, I roll off of her and rest my hand on my chest and then a terrifying thought pops into my mind. "Please tell me you're on birth control."

I see her look over at me in my peripheral. "Yes," she says, sounding satiated.

I shut my eyes. "Thank fuck."

"Are you… Have you been safe?" she asks. I look over at her. "I mean, I know this wasn't your first time." She looks concerned, and a little hurt.

"No man would go bare with the women at the clubhouse."

She nods, looking up at the ceiling.

"Hey," I say, grabbing her hand. "You know none of them fucking mattered. Nothing I've done before this fucking meant anything."

She gives me a shy smile. "Was it good for you?"

I smirk. "Yeah, Bexley." I sit up. "Come on. I'm sure you've got some bleeding going on. We need a shower."

She blushes. "God, just throw it out there."

"What? It's life. Who gives a shit?" I walk into the bathroom, pulling back the shower curtain and turning on the water as she walks in. "After you." I gesture. She smiles, stepping in.

Paige P. Horne

The house is outdated. This bathroom could really use a remodel, but she doesn't seem to care. I got a good deal on it since it was a foreclosure. It came as is, though. Figured it could be a weekend project or some shit. The stuff I can't do I'll just hire someone.

Bexley wraps her hair up so it doesn't get wet, and she grabs the soap, washing her body before handing it to me. I rub my chest with it, looking down the length of her as suds run over her skin.

God, she's beautiful. I'm getting hard just standing in front of her.

She notices. "You wanna go again?"

I look down, rubbing my soapy hand over my cock. "Can you?"

"Eh, kinda sore. But I could try something else?"

I lift a brow. "You wanna give me a blow job?"

She licks her lips, looking shy. It's cute as hell.

"Be my guest," I say. She moves us so I'm under the water, rinsing the soap off of me. She bends, going down on her knees. "Wait," I say. I reach and grab a washcloth from the cabinet beside the shower and toss it down. "Your knees will thank me." I wink.

She smirks, grabbing it and putting in under her knees. Her small hand wraps around my dick, and as soon as her mouth opens to let me in, I flex my hips, groaning in satisfaction. "Pretend it's a

Genesis

Popsicle on a hot summer day, and I'll come in minutes," I tell her.

She smiles over my cock, and I moan.

"God, girl. You have no idea what you're doing to me." I grasp her pulled up hair.

Bexley does what I say or either she's done this before. She sucks me until my knees want to give out, and I explode in her mouth, which results in a scrunched up nose from her. I laugh as she stands and puts her face under the water, clearly not swallowing.

"That's pretty fucking gross," she says.

"Eh, you'll get used to it." I smack her ass and kiss her forehead. "Come on. Let's ride for a while."

After we dress and I lock the house up, we climb back in the truck. I reach over, grabbing a joint out of the glove compartment. Bexley watches me intriguingly. "What are you doing?" she asks.

"What does it look like?" I reply, lighting the weed.

Her tongue goes to the roof of her mouth in curiosity.

"Want a hit?' I ask.

She reaches for it. I hold my finger up. Taking another toke, I grab her chin, pull her face to mine, and blow into her mouth. "Hold it in," I tell her. She does and then releases on a cough.

Paige P. Horne

I smile at her, start the truck, and place the joint between my lips. I roll the window down—enough to keep the smell out—before reaching up and turning the knob on the stereo when I hear Bone Thugs-N-Harmony saying it's the first of the month.

We cruise down the road, and I let Bexley hit the joint one more time before I toss the thing. She grins and I'm pretty sure she's buzzed.

I laugh. "You high?"

"I don't know," she says, giggling.

I smile, looking back at the road. We ride, listening to music, and I tell her my plans about remodeling the house. She tells me where she's going to college when she graduates and says she's already taking college courses.

"That's good, Bexley. I'm proud of you."

"Thanks," she says. "Oh, I love this song." She turns up the volume.

"What the hell is this?'" I ask.

"'Mr. Brightside,'" she says.

I lift a brow.

"The Killers?" she questions. "You don't know The Killers?"

"I know a lot of killers," I reply.

She frowns, hitting me in my chest. I act like it hurt.

"Not funny."

"It was a little funny," I say, catching her hiding a smile. She rolls her eyes and dances in the seat,

Genesis

singing and puckering her lips at me when the lead singer croons *it was only a kiss.* I chuckle at her, looking back at the road, thinking I've never been happier.

Chapter Twenty-One

Bexley
Five days missing

"Bexley, you're not going to die."

"How can you say that?" I ask him as I push off the wall and sniff, rubbing my nose across my cotton-covered shoulder. "We're out in the middle of nowhere. Who's going to find us out here? We have no phone, no water, nothing. Oh, wait." I cluck my tongue. "We do have a complete psychopath who wants to kill everyone you love, including me, because of something you did, which you have no clue about. Am I correct on that?"

He nods. "You're correct."

"Do you even have a notion? I mean, this is big. This man has gone through a lot of trouble. Surely something you've done in the past comes to mind?"

He shakes his head, looking up for a moment. "Nothing."

"Hmm." I nod sarcastically and lean my head back against the wall.

This man.

He probably has no idea because he's done so much shit he can't keep count. There's no telling how many enemies he has. I exhale defeat as my stomach growls even though the man gave us both a

Genesis

few bites of food. It's shit, though. It does nothing to help give us energy. In only a few days, we've both lost weight, and fatigue is so strong at this point, I could sleep for ages.

"Can you stand up?" he asks me.

"Well, I've gone to the bathroom, so I know I can walk, but my legs are killing me."

"Well, get on with it then."

"Don't be pushy," I scowl.

He exhales, pulling his shoulders back as I lean against the wall and slowly slide up it. My muscles are tired, my bones shaky. I wince as I stretch them out and make them hold my weight just like I do every time the stranger takes me to the bathroom.

You know how when you sleep on your arms wrong for a while and it hurts to move them? Yeah, this shit is ten times worse than that. When you stop using your body as much as it's used to, it becomes weak.

I clench my teeth and hurry up the wall. "Good girl," Danny says once I'm up straight.

I scoff. "Don't say that. I'm not a fucking kid."

"I didn't mean it that way, Bexley. Jesus Christ, Hail Mary." He rolls his eyes. "Come here," he says. "Walk to me."

It takes me a moment, but I gather myself and take small steps toward him, grimacing as I do. My bones creak, and my hips protest and pop.

"I'm never sitting again."

He chuckles. "I've got to get out of this chair, too." Danny's chair is not the same as mine. His is iron, while mine is wood. The only way he can get out is if we cut the zip ties around his wrists, arms, and legs.

"Okay, I'm here," I say.

"Turn around and bend. I'll lean up as much as I can. There's a knife on my hip."

"What? A knife? You still wear that?"

My mind flies back to almost losing my virginity to this man, before, ya know, actually losing my virginity to this man. I remember the knife he wore on his hip. He always wore it. "Why are you just now telling me this?" I spin around, almost tumbling over.

"Careful," he says. "Okay, back up. It's on my belt on the left side."

I reach for him, feeling the softness of his shirt. I pull it up and feel for the knife.

"Fuck," he says. "I thought it might be gone. That's why I didn't say anything."

I stand up straight and turn back to look at him.

He shakes his head, his brow furrowing. "This guy does know me. He knows me well enough to know I wear a knife. Fuck!" he says again.

I flinch and take a step back. Danny rubs his chin over his shoulder, looking around. I see the dried blood on his temple and down the side of his face.

"Does that hurt?" I ask, pointing at my chin.

Genesis

"What?" He realizes what I'm talking about. "Oh, that. No."

I look down at where I lifted his shirt to get the knife, seeing bruising. "What about that?"

He looks down. "It's fine, love."

I freeze in place at the term of endearment he just used for me. I feel as though the ground tilts, the walls shift, and my balance gets thrown to the wind.

My husband only called me Bexley or Bex, which was fine. But Danny called me love, and it always, always made me melt. I should be mad at him. I should hate him so much, but my heart just won't let me.

"Fuck, I'm sorry," he says, shaking his head. "I know you hate me. I shouldn't have called you that."

"I don't hate you, Danny. I hate what you did to me, to us."

He looks up at me, his eyes tired as lines web out from them. Danny's no longer a boy. No, that's for sure. He's a man, and this lifestyle he's chosen has aged him.

He's still as handsome as ever, though, just a little rougher looking. More tattoos, more scars.

But the same person I've always loved.

I look around, not wanting to get sucked into the force that is *us*. "There's got to be something in here that can cut these off." I go about looking, leaving him alone with his thoughts, even though there's only a bathroom and a bedroom to disappear to.

Chapter Twenty-Two
Bexley
2003

I wake with a huge stretch from the best sleep I've had in weeks. Last night, when I came in after a long kiss from Danny that almost ended up going farther until he reluctantly forced me out the truck door, I snuck into the kitchen and grabbed a bag of Chips Ahoy! cookies and a big glass of milk. I ate until I threw up, and then passed out in my bed. I'd never been hungrier.

And I've never, ever been happier. I brush my hair and teeth, splash my face with cold water, and put on a little makeup before sliding into a pair of jeans and a sweater. Heading down to the kitchen, I see Uncle Hale is already up, drinking his coffee while he watches the morning news.

"Good morning," I say.

"Morning," he replies. "There was a drive-by shooting near your old neighborhood."

I reach for a glass in the cabinet and walk over to the fridge. "Really? Was anyone hurt?" I ask, grabbing the orange juice.

"No. Witnesses say they saw a '96 Impala with bullet holes and busted windows, though." He looks back at me with inquiring eyes.

My heart liquefies in my chest, pooling at the bottom of my stomach.

"Isn't that the same car your boyfriend drives?" he asks.

"Yeah, but how many of those exist?" I say, shrugging it off as I grab a piece of cheese toast he already cooked. "Besides, his is in the shop. Something about the radiator busting." And that's the second time I've lied to this man.

"Oh," he says. "Well, that's good."

"Yeah." I smile and take a sip of my juice before walking into the living room. "I gotta head to school," I say. "See you later."

"Trinity will be over again for dinner. If you want to join us, that would be nice."

"Okay," I say.

"Love ya, kid. Be safe."

"Ditto," I reply, putting the toast in my mouth as I grab my keys and books from the table by the door and head out.

I shut my car door a little harder than normal. Danny lied to me. I know that was his car. It's too fucking coincidental. I start the car, checking the back seat to make sure I have a coat.

This is going to be a long day.

I get through the morning and lunch, and by the end of the day, I'm still thinking about Danny and his lies. I just lost my virginity to this guy, I told him I loved him, and he lied to me so easily. I'm

Genesis

closing my locker when I turn and see Samuel in his basketball shorts and a white T-shirt.

"Hey," he says. God, he looks cute.

"Hey. Got practice?"

"Yeah, wanna come?" he replies. I bite my lip with narrowed eyes as I think on it. I don't really want to go home right now. Danny might pop up, and I'm not ready to face him just yet.

"Why not? I'll do my homework, too."

"Cool," he says.

Samuel is into all the sports. Basketball, baseball—you name it, he does it. I picture Danny in a baseball uniform. It's like John Travolta in *Grease*. It just doesn't fit, and it makes me laugh.

"What's funny?" Samuel asks.

"Nothing," I say, waving it off. "How have you been? I haven't seen much of you lately."

"Busy," he says. "Between practice and the new job, I don't have much time for anything else."

"What job did you get?"

"I started building houses. You know Teller from the baseball team?"

"Yeah." I nod.

"His dad runs a construction crew, and he got me a job."

"Cool."

He shrugs. "I like it. Makes me feel good to know I've helped build someone a home."

I smile. "You're such a great guy, Samuel."

He looks down at me. All the O'Brien boys are tall. I feel so small next to them. We head down the hall to the school gym where I already hear basketballs being dribbled.

"So, you and Danny been hanging out a lot?" he says.

"Yeah," I reply.

"You two a couple now?"

I shrug. "Maybe."

"Maybe?"

"It's complicated."

His brow furrows. "Why is it complicated?"

I exhale. "I don't know. It just is. Danny's—"

"An asshole?" Samuel says as his eyebrows rise.

I smirk. "He can be."

We stop before we walk through the doors of the gym and he looks at me. "Look, it's none of my business, and he's my brother, so that means you're off-limits to me now, but you should be with someone who's got a better future for himself. We both know Danny hangs out with a tough crowd."

"He does," I agree. "But I care about him."

"He cares about you, too, but so do I. Just be careful, Bexley. I'm always here if you need me."

"Thanks." I smile. "You better go in. I'll be on the blenchers."

He nods.

Genesis

I watch Samuel jog into the gym with the rest of his team, thinking about his words. *He cares about you, but so do I.*

I love Samuel for that. He's so sweet. I head in myself, watching the guys practice for a bit before I get my books out and do my homework.

Chapter Twenty-Three

Bones
Nine days missing

"Where the fuck is she?"

I'm jolted awake from sleeping with my head against the wall. The stranger barges into the cabin, his heavy boots hitting the hard floor.

"Calm the fuck down. Like she could go anywhere," I say with an eye roll. Damn, I need a smoke, and a drink would be nice. "Hey, why don't you bring me a pack of cigarillos next time you come, yeah?"

The man stalks toward me. Raring back, he punches me in the face. Not once, but twice and I'm out.

Chapter Twenty-Four
Danny
2003

I stand at the scrapyard, watching as they crush my car. I didn't report the damage to my insurance company because there would be too many questions, and the guy I got to look at the car said it would cost more to fix the shit than the thing was worth. They fucked my engine and the top frame. How we didn't get popped beats the hell out of me.

I hit my cigarette as the man gives me some cash for the car, and then I turn and climb into Johnny's. "What now?" he asks.

"Now I gotta find another ride." I toss my smoke and shut the car door, looking at the time on the radio. It's early still. Maybe I'll swing by Bexley's school after I get a new car and surprise her. Take her to eat or something. I haven't stop thinking about her all day. Yesterday was one of the best days of my life. She doesn't know how happy she makes me.

"How's the new apartment?" I ask Johnny as we head down the road.

"Fine. Carson is going to have to get out soon, though. He's messy as hell."

I laugh.

"What car lot you wanna go to?" he asks.

"The one on Cotton Avenue. At the corner."

"All right. You paying cash?"

"Yeah. If they got anything worth a shit. If not, we'll have to go across town."

Johnny reaches for his cigarettes and Zippo lighter.

"Did I tell you I talked to Officer Radcliff a while back?"

Johnny lights his smoke. "No."

"Motherfucker told me Warren sends his regards. These cops around here abuse their power."

"In a way, it's a good thing," Johnny says.

I look over at him questionably.

He shrugs, letting his window down a bit. "If they weren't crooked, you and I would be in prison."

I scoff. "You're probably right."

We pass through town, riding under bridges and seeing the homeless sleep alongside big black trash bags against the fences we pass.

"Has Moretti said what he wants to do about Warren and his men?" Johnny asks me.

"Not yet. But I'm sure he's thinking on it. Whatever we do, it's got to be a surprise for them. They can't know we're coming."

"Yeah," he agrees, and that's all we say about that.

Genesis

The day moves along, and after we go to a few car lots, I finally find a 1985 Chevy Monte Carlo I have to have.

The guy nearly shits his pants when I give him cash for the thing. I call my insurance company from a pay phone and get it switched over, and then I part ways with Johnny, telling him I'll meet him later at the clubhouse. On my way to Bexley's school, I think about the conversation we had on Thanksgiving.

It's the sweet ones that win eventually. With that thought, I stop by the local flower shop and buy her some roses. I'm pulling into the full parking lot a little after three as high schoolers stand around each other's cars talking shit about their day and whatever else. A bunch of kids chase each other with snowballs, laughing and almost busting their ass on the slick ground.

A feeling I don't care for swarms in my chest. Maybe I missed out. I never gave school a chance, always ready to get out and run the streets. Once I park the car, I look over, seeing a make-out session in the back seat of an older Honda. I exhale, wondering what it would be like to walk out of the school with Bexley, holding her hand so all these little fuckers knew she was mine.

And then I burst out laughing. I didn't miss out on shit. These kids have no fucking clue what real life is. When they leave here, they'll be forced to get dead-end jobs, saving up every penny they can for when they finally get ready to retire, while I've already made enough to leave all this behind if I really wanted to. I've been putting money under my mattress since I was thirteen. My only big spends were two cars and a house, and I still have enough cash to live off of for a while without earning another penny.

But it's not even about the money for me. It's the thrill of saying fuck the rules. I'll live how I choose and not how society thinks I should. No body owns you. You don't come into this world with a rulebook that has a checklist you must follow.

Go to school.
Graduate.
Get a job.
Save.
Get married.
Buy a house
Have kids.
Raise them.
Retire.
Grow old.

Reminisce about your life until regret fills your chest like congestive heart failure because you didn't do what you wanted but what everyone else expected out of you.

Fuck that.

Genesis

I look toward the school doors, waiting for her to walk out, but she doesn't, and half the parking lot is empty now.

"Where the hell is she?"

One by one more cars leave, and then I see Samuel's car he got from our parents' life insurance money that Ma put to the side for all of us.

I know he plays basketball, along with every other fucking sport. I hop out of the car, grabbing a smoke before lighting it. Walking to the gym, I lift my hoodie to keep the wind off my neck. I pass schoolgirls who give me flirty smiles, and just for the fuck of it, I smile back. They freak out and giggle amongst themselves, which makes me roll my eyes.

"Isn't that Danny O'Brien?" one says.

"Yeah, that's Samuel's brother," another says.

How the hell do they know me in this school?

I look back at them, hitting my smoke one more time before tossing it and shrugging, then grabbing the handle on the gym door. My eyes search the space, and then I see Bexley sitting on the bottom bleacher. Samuel rests his foot on the bench beside her, tying his shoe. She's smiling at him, and he says something that causes her to playfully hit his shoulder.

I don't fucking like it.

I push the hoodie off my head, walking toward them. Bexley sees me first, and her expression changes from happy to sad.

She isn't glad to see me?

Samuel notices and turns his head. He drops his foot and stands up straight.

"What's up, brother?" he says.

I lift my chin. "What's up?"

I look down at Bexley who doesn't say anything. "Hey, Bexley," I say in a *you can't speak?* way.

"Hey," she says. She closes her textbook.

"Shouldn't you be practicing?" I ask Samuel.

He narrows his eyes. "She's allowed to talk to people, Danny."

"Did I say she wasn't?" I raise my brow at him.

"Whatever," he says. "Remember what I said, Bexley." He looks down at her.

My eye twitches. "What did you say?"

He ignores me and runs back onto the court. Fucker.

"What did he say?" I ask the girl who's obviously mad at me. Shouldn't I be the one who's mad? She's flirting with a boy she knows likes her and it's my goddamn brother.

She shoves her books into her bag before standing up.

"Yo, are you gonna answer me?" I ask. She gives me a look that says no before she puts her bag over her shoulder and walks toward the exit, looking out

Genesis

at Samuel, who's watching when he should be worried about the fucking ball and not my girl.

When she opens the door, the cold air replaces the warmth of the gym instantly.

"Bexley," I say. She keeps walking, so I reach out and grab her arm, turning her to face me. "What the fuck is this?" I ask. "You staying after school to watch my brother practice basketball?"

"So what?" she says.

"She speaks," I say sarcastically as my eyes widen. "He's my fucking brother, that's what. And you know he likes you. You were flirting with him."

"What?" she says like that's the most ridiculous thing she's ever said. "I was talking to him, Danny. I talk to the opposite sex all day. You think I'm flirting with them, too?"

I run a hand over my chin. "What's gotten into you? Huh?" A few people walk by, so I lower my voice and dip my hands into my hoodie's pockets. "Did I fuck up somehow? Are you regretting yesterday?" I hate the way I sound right now. I'm fucking Danny O'Brien, and I'm acting like a hurt bitch because Bexley's mad at me, when I should be the one mad at her.

Her face softens. "No," she says with a shake of her head.

Air leaves my lungs in a relieved exhale, but I don't make it noticeable to her.

"Then what's wrong?"

"You lied. That's what's wrong." She puts hair behind her ear, her cheeks turning a rosy shade of pink from the cold.

"Lied?" I ask.

"Your car. It's not in the shop, is it?"

The ground rocks beneath my feet. I narrow my eyes. "Who told you any differently?"

"The news, Danny. I heard it on the news this morning before school. Witnesses saw it get shot up from a drive-by, and you know who else saw it? My uncle."

Some teachers walk by, and I drag my hand from my nose to my mouth. "Can we talk about this somewhere else?"

"I don't know," she says.

"You don't know?"

She looks distraught and second-guessing herself.

"Danny, I…" she pauses, and my chest sinks as she swallows the words she didn't say.

She's changing her mind. This is too much for her, and fuck, why wouldn't it be? I look past her, my sight catching the gray clouds hovering in the distance, and a cold, cold wind rushes around us as the world I thought I was building crashes in on me. Disappointment is a bitter, sick taste in my throat, and heartache is new.

I reach over and take her hand. "Come on," I say.

Genesis

Nearly tripping over her feet to keep up with me, she follows almost at my side, but more behind to my newish car, and when I open the door for her to get in, she glares back at me.

"I just bought it."

She exhales, shaking her head as she gets in. I shut the door and walk over to the other side. I start the engine so we can have some heat. Her eyes are on the dash, blinking slowly.

The roses.

"I got you those," I say with a shrug.

Her face falls. The mad fades, and in its place is an affection she only shows me.

"You said you wanted a sweet guy, so, I'm trying."

She brings the flowers to her face and breathes in, looking at them. "Being sweet isn't the problem here, Danny," she says hopelessly. "What if you were in the car when they drove by? What if they had killed you?"

"I wasn't, though."

"But you could have been. What if I had been in there with you?"

I don't respond, only look to the steering wheel. My heart doesn't want to agree with her, but my mind knows she's right. She's unbending and stubborn as hell. I look at the girl I care about. The girl who let me be her first, the one I can't stop thinking about.

"I'm not sure what you want me to say here, love."

Her eyes dip to the floor, and mine jump to the window when I see snow start to fall around us.

"I told you who I was. I gave you a chance to change your mind."

"And now it's too late?" she asks. "Why does it have to be this way? Why can't you stop?"

"I'd never ask you to stop being who you are. Don't ask that of me."

"Who you are is dangerous. You're going to get yourself killed. I won't be able to handle it, Danny." She starts crying and her tears are caustic, burning my beating muscle.

"The car was parked, Bexley. It was parked and I wasn't in it. They knew that. They didn't shoot to kill me. It was a warning."

"A warning? Good God, like that makes it better." She looks heavenward, like there's some kind of answer there.

"Well, I'm not dead," I say, like that *does* make it better.

She wipes her face, rubbing her finger over one of the rose petals.

"I'm not going to let anything happen to you, and nothing's going to happen to me. Trust me."

She looks at me with wet lashes and pouty lips.

I reach over and take her hand, running my fingers over the bracelet I gave her. What this girl

Genesis

fails to understand is, she no longer has a choice in the matter of us. She told me she loved me. She gave herself to me. It's done. I'll be damned if I'm going to let anything come between us now.

I bring her soft knuckles to my lips, kissing them lightly, and then I drop her hand, putting the car in neutral. I back us out of here and head to my house.

"Where are we going?" she asks.

"My house."

I don't ask her if she has plans, and she doesn't protest. She looks out the window as we drive away from the north side of town, rubbing the rose petals in her own thoughts. I wish I knew what she was thinking, but part of me does. She's worried. She's wondering what she should do.

She's young. Hell, I'm young, but I know I want her. I also know I'm being selfish. Deep inside, past my cold soul, is a little mass of reason. She should be with someone who doesn't risk her life just by being with them.

But I'm a prick and an asshole, so I shut the door on that thought as we drive down the driveway. Snow crunches beneath my tires, and the lake is all but frozen over.

I yank the car in park, and we climb out, her with the flowers still in her hands. I unlock the door, take the roses, and place them on the table before grabbing her to me. My heart rushes for a girl whose eyes melt when I touch her. I run my nose alongside hers. The chaos of the world settles, and everything out there doesn't fucking matter.

The smallest note leaves her lungs, filtering into me, proving to me that she can't stop this either. No matter if she thinks it's wrong, it's too late for her, too. My hands find the backs of her thighs, and my mouth connects with hers as I lift her up. She hooks her arms around my neck, pulling me down, and I open her mouth with mine.

My nervous system catches fire when she rocks her hips, searching for friction. My tongue licks, and my teeth bite as the coldness from outside dissolves. My skin thaws from being so close to her. Moving to the back of the house where she let me have all of her, I turn into the bedroom and pull the comforter back, revealing clean sheets I changed last night after I dropped her off. My knees bend, and I lay her down, my hand going up her sweater, running over her rib cage and across her bra.

I grab a handful of her breast as her cadence matches mine. I pull the sweater up more, bending so I can kiss her stomach and across her ribs. I pull her bra cup down and capture her nipple, sucking and licking, looking up as she looks down. Her chest rises, then falls quickly. Her pupils widen in the low-lit room, and her heart beats erratically against me.

She sits up, cradling my cheeks and stealing my kiss. We go deeper, cling tighter. I let go, pulling

Genesis

my hoodie and shirt over my head as she tosses her sweater and then her bra next to the soft black cotton.

I grab her again, kissing her jaw, up to her ear, breathing her in as she goes for my jeans. I slide my shoes off and my jeans go with them as she lifts her hips and does the same. Almost naked in my bed, she spreads her legs and pulls me down on top of her, gasping when she feels how much I want her.

"Tell me you love me," I say, creating a tempo with my hips.

She shakes.

"Tell me you'll never leave," I breathe as I take her earlobe into my mouth, sucking.

She doesn't answer the second question and it hurts, but I can't think about that right now.

"I love you," she says.

I smile sadly, covering her mouth with mine. Reaching down, I rub her clit through her soaked panties.

Her heavy lids shut, and our lips stay close, touching slightly as her breathing speeds up with every rub of my fingers. I shift back. Pulling down her panties, I kiss the inside of her knee as I slip them over her painted pink toes. She goes to shut her thighs, but I stop her.

She groans as I run my fingers between her lips and bundle of earth-shattering nerves. I grab myself, dragging my hand down my length as I sit up on my knees. She watches with half-moon eyes. I move up, grabbing her thighs, looking down at her as I slide inside slowly. Her eyes shut from pleasure as she grabs the pillow above her head. My jaw tightens, and my heart pounds with hope, love, pain, and an ache that I know will get worse when she wises up.

I fold, dropping my hands beside her head, and I move. Her ankles link behind my back, and she exhales beautifully. I rock into her with a steady beat, leaning down to kiss her breast, sucking the skin until it breaks. Her fingers go in my hair as I fuck her.

"Did you think it would be like this?" she asks me.

"I had an idea," I reply.

She smiles, knocking emotion from my chest. "I love you, Bexley." Her smile fades, and in its place is a heartfelt wonder. Her lips lie open, my pace slows, and she feels so fucking good, I could die.

She sits up, causing me to hit deeper. Her hand goes to my nape and she pulls me to her, kissing my lips, running her nose against mine. My stroke speeds up as her back hits the mattress and her nails find my skin. I put my face in the crook of her neck, pushing into her with a steady beat.

"I'm about to come," I tell her.

Genesis

She doesn't respond, but sinks her teeth into my shoulder. Her legs tremble and I grasp the sheets as I let go with a rush of breath from my lungs.

I breathe heavy, feeling my dick throb inside of her before I pull out. I move and lie down on my back, looking up at the ceiling and shutting my eyes as my heart slows.

She puts her hand on my chest and I grab it in mine, holding it as she snuggles beside me.

"I had an idea, too," she says. My eyes jump down to her and I laugh. I wish I could bottle this moment up because dread is knowing one day I won't have it.

I bring her closer, and then we get up and shower before I take her back to her car.

"What am I going to tell my uncle about your new car?" she says when we pull into the school parking lot.

I shrug. "Tell him it was my car that got shot up."

"I can't tell him that, Danny. Besides, I already lied and said yours was in the shop."

I scratch the back of my neck. "Shit," I say, shifting the car into neutral as I pull the emergency brake up. "Well, how about you meet me outside for a while until it blows over?"

"Guess I'll have to. He'll wonder why you're not picking me up, though."

"I'm sure you can think of something," I say.

She shrugs. "Yeah. I'll just tell him I stopped seeing you."

"You can tell him anything you want, but don't fucking tell him that."

She rolls her eyes. "Whatever." She opens her car door.

"Hey," I say. She looks back at me. "I'm sorry I put you in this situation. I don't want you having to lie to your uncle."

She sighs. "It's okay. Like you said, I'll figure it out."

I nod. "Call me later."

"Okay."

I wait for her to get into her car and reverse before I follow. We then go separate ways once we pull out.

Chapter Twenty-Five

Bexley
Ten days missing

Danny was knocked out for a full hour after the stranger hit him. His wrists are bloody and cut to pieces from him trying to get loose. I can't imagine what his arms look like underneath that shirt. I got dragged into the living room, or whatever you want to call it. There's no furniture in here. I've been looking out the window in the bedroom, trying to see any sign of a road or cars or something.

He actually let me stay free, though. He fed me and left. I feel like this guy is regretting things, like he forgets himself, and then remembers why we're here in the first place. I can't help but wonder how close he was to Danny.

Did he work with him every day? Has he known him for years, or was it just someone Danny crossed paths with? But then, I think about the knife. You'd only know Danny carried if you saw him with his shirt off.

He left some food for Danny and told me to figure out how to give it to him. It wasn't easy, but we got the job done. He actually left us some water bottles, too, which is odd. Like I said, I feel like this guy is having second thoughts or something.

It's late. I'm not sure of the time, but it just feels late. I look out the window, which I discovered was nailed shut from the outside, and the door is locked from the outside, too, hence why he left me untethered to something.

Danny's face is bruised, and his lip and nose are busted now. My lip is still sore from where he slapped me, and my jaw is surely bruised. We're pretty banged up, but we're alive and we have each other.

"Danny," I say into the moonlight as I look up at the sparkling stars. That's the only thing I'll say good about this place. There's no smog, so you can see every last twinkle.

"Yeah?" he says.

"Remember that Christmas we spent together? How you surprised me with the lights?"

"Hmm," he says in remembrance. "I remember your face."

"My face?" I ask.

"Yeah."

"Ah, that's right. You did say that."

"That's all I wanted for Christmas was to see you happy. I tried so hard to make you happy."

I turn to look at him—this strong man, beaten and tied to a chair. Malnourished and void of energy.

"I was happy. If only for a moment, I was happy."

Chapter Twenty-Six

Bexley
2003

"Don't look," he says to me. I laugh, holding my hands over my eyes because I can't trust myself to not open them. He parks the car and I hear him hop out before my door opens. He grabs my arm, helping me out of the car.

"Okay, stand right here," he says, positioning me. He lets go and then says, "Open."

I move my hands, opening my eyes. A slow smile spreads through my eyes and across my lips as I scan over the house. Lights hang around the top and outline the windows, and in the front there's an enormous Christmas tree.

"You did this?" I ask.

He shrugs. "I hired someone."

I laugh and hit his chest. "That's cheating."

He grins, catching my hand and pulling me to him. "But I did it with the best of intentions. I really wanted to see your face. I'd give all my money to see that look."

My eyes linger on his as his thumb strokes my own. His lips part and his other hand anchors on my hip.

"Come on," he says, breaking the spell he has me under. "I know you'll be with your uncle tomorrow for Christmas, so I figured we'd have our own here."

"You know you're invited over," I tell him.

"I'll come over," he says simply. I smile because that really makes me happy.

I hold on to his upper arm as we head inside. My eyes widen when I look at the Christmas tree filled with small gifts under it.

"Danny," I say, looking up at him. "What is this?"

"It's yours," he says, biting his inner cheek. "Although, I may have gone a little overboard."

"Ya think?" I reply, releasing his arm so I can walk over and look. "I don't have you anything. Well, I do, but it's at my house."

"You didn't have to buy anything for me."

I roll my eyes. "Well, I'm fucking glad I did." I look back at the pretty wrapped gifts. "You hire someone?" I ask with a smirk.

He lifts his shoulder, walking to the fridge and grabbing a bottle of champagne. "Let's have a drink or two, and then you can open all of your presents."

I exhale. "I don't feel right about this. What am I going to tell my uncle?"

"Nothing. This stuff is for you here."

"What? For me here?"

Genesis

"Yeah, so you have some shit. Maybe, every once in a while, you can tell your uncle you're staying at a friend's house and stay here instead?"

"Danny," I say gently. "I'm only sixteen. We can't pretend live together."

His brow furrows. "Who said anything about living together? I just mean when you want to wash your hair, you can blow dry it or whatever. There're some gift cards for clothes and whatever else you want to buy. I got you some jewelry, too, and Bath and Body Works shit."

"You picked all this out?" I ask suspiciously.

He lowers his head. "I may have gotten some help."

I cross my arms. "From whom?"

"Don't worry 'bout it." He pops the top on the champagne, and I laugh when it flies across the room and some shoots out the top.

I grab the glasses on the counter and slide them over to him. "I am worried about it."

"Fine. The girls at the clubhouse."

I cock my head. "Seriously?"

"*What*? They're girls. They know what you all like." He waves a hand like it's that simple.

"We don't all like the same stuff, dummy."

He fills the glasses, handing me mine. "Did I fuck up again?"

I shake my head, rolling my eyes at this clueless boy that I love. I know his heart was in the right place, so how can I be mad that he asked a few clubhouse hookers to help him Christmas shop for his girlfriend?

God, just thinking those words makes me question myself. I fiddle with my earring. "You didn't fuck up entirely."

His lip lifts. "I'll take it."

We clink glasses and I chuckle before I take a sip of the bubbly. "Better than beer," I say with a look of approval.

He taps his hand on the counter. "All right, let me see you smile," he says, walking over to the tree.

Christmas morning equals warm pj's, hot cocoa, and *A Christmas Story* on repeat for most of the day. Uncle Hale and I exchange gifts, and Trinity comes over in the afternoon, but the sun goes down without a word from Danny. "I thought Danny was coming over?" Uncle Hale says as I grab a drink from the fridge.

"He got tied up with family stuff," I say on a shrug, like it's no big deal, like what I'm saying is true.

Genesis

And that's the third time I've lied to him about Danny. I look to the TV when the local news comes on.

"It seems a bad batch of heroin has been floating around Postings over the past couple of months. We caught up with a local medic to see what he had to say about this."

"Every week there seems to be more and more overdoses on the streets. It's becoming an epidemic."

Jesus, this town.

"All right, well, you're more than welcome to watch a movie with us," Hale says.

"That's sweet, but I'll let you two have some time."

"We don't mind," Trinity says from the couch. "We've got popcorn."

I give her a smile. "You kids have fun."

"Suit yourself," Hale says.

I walk back to my room, shutting the door behind me as I grab the phone from my bed and dial the O'Briens' number again.

"Hello," Ma says on the other end of the phone.

"Hey, Ma, he made it home yet?" I ask her.

"Sorry, Bexley. No."

I nod even though she can't see me.

"Is that her again?" I hear. "Let me talk to her." I hear some shuffling, and then Samuel's voice comes on the other end of the line. "Bexley. Why don't you come over? Ma would love to see you, and Paul's here."

I look through the photos I took from my new digital camera Danny bought me. I captured Hale and Trinity playing in the snow and a redbird landing on a snow-covered tree. I really like this thing.

I don't really like him right now, though.

I hear Hale and Trinity laughing from the living room. "Okay," I find myself saying. "Be there soon."

I pull a beanie over my head and grab my coat from the back of my vanity chair, slipping the camera in its pocket. Opening my bedroom door, I walk out, sliding my arms through my coat. "Hey, I'm heading over to a friend's. I'll be back later."

"What friend?" Hale asks.

"Amanda from my study group. She got a bunch of nail polish and stuff, so we're gonna do pedicures and talk about sex and boys." I tease.

He scrunches his nose. "Have fun with that," he says with an eye roll.

I laugh. "Bye."

Disappointment swims heavy in my chest, mixing with an ache I can't touch as I ride over to the south side of Postings. He could be hurt, or he could be just hanging out with his friends at the clubhouse. Hell, who knows what he's doing. But

Genesis

the fact that he hasn't bothered to call me all day really, really hurts. Like crying hurts.

I grip the steering wheel as Counting Crows croons from my radio's speakers. My thoughts run like the wind, and before I know it, I'm not going the right way, but heading to the lake house. I decide I better call Samuel and let him know I'm not coming so he won't worry.

I put a few quarters into the pay phone and dial their number. Waiting for them to answer, I run my finger over the cord, leaning back against the phone stand.

"Hello?" Paul says.

I clear my throat. "Hey," I say. "Um, look, I'm not really feeling it tonight. I'm just going to stay home."

"Then why aren't you calling from your house?" he asks me.

I sigh, guessing he even knows my number from the caller ID by now. "I just decided to go for a ride."

"You all right, Bexley?"

I nod, swallowing the lump in my throat. "Yeah."

He's silent for a moment, and I hear the door click shut in the back.

"He can't help it, you know?"

"Who can't help what?"

"Danny. He's just like our dad. It's just the way he is. You need to make a choice, Bex. You need to decide what kind of life you want. Danny will always be married to the streets. You'll always be wondering where he is or if he's coming home. You can't change that."

A tear rolls down my cheek. "I know. It just hurts," I say as my voice cracks. "It's fucking Christmas, Paul. He hasn't even called." A weight leaves my chest because, God, I needed someone to talk to about this, but I've had no one.

"That guy he's working for probably has him tied up. The men he surrounds himself with… you don't just tell them no, Bexley. Doesn't matter what holiday it is."

I look out at the tree line as the wind blows snow across the road. I pull my coat tighter on an exhale, rubbing my nose.

"Look, I know he's my brother and I love the guy more than anything, but I love you, too. You're Little Girl," he says. "I don't want you hurt. Do what makes you happy. Life's too short to settle for just enough."

"Okay," I say as sadness rivers down my face. I sniff and my chest shudders.

"Get home. It's too cold out."

"I will," I say.

"Merry Christmas, Bex."

Genesis

"Yeah, you, too. Hey, Paul," I say before I hang up.

"Yeah?"

"Thanks."

"Anytime," he says. "You're family."

My eyes close as the ground sways below my feet. Gravity seems heavier, and life seems broken.

"Okay, bye." I hang the phone up so he doesn't hear me cry, and it takes my change. I put a hand over my mouth as tears blur my vision.

Heartache tastes sick. I walk away from the phone. Climbing into my car, I start the motor and stare out at the road as cars pass by.

We always have a choice.

And I guess I'm an idiot. Knowing I should go home, I don't. I put the car in drive, and I head to the lake house because I'd rather be without him there than at home.

Stupid, stupid girl.

Chapter Twenty-Seven

Bones
Sixteen days missing

When do they stop looking for a missing person? Surely the case has gone cold by now. One minute we were walking down the street, and the next we vanished. How did I not beat this man? How have I not gotten out of here?

He took the pieces of Bexley's broken chair, or I would have told her to break a window and use the glass to cut this shit off of me. There's nothing in this house. It's void of any furniture besides the chair I'm sitting on. God, this fucking chair. I'm going to beat him to death with it when I get free.

I've already got it planned out. I'll tie a zip tie around his throat just enough to let the tiniest of air through. And then I beat him in the face repeatedly with the iron chair until it breaks every fucking tiny bone. I'll let him sit here for days like that, and then I'll come back and break other bones. He'll bleed internally.

It'll be one of the best moments of my life.

I look over at Bexley as she lies on the floor with her arms still tied behind her back. She's grown thinner. Her face is still busted. I can't save her. I

Genesis

can't do anything but sit in this godforsaken chair. How many days has it been? Fifteen, sixteen maybe? I'm not even sure anymore. They're all blurring together.

My legs are numb, and my arms and back feel nearly broken. I've stared out the windows enough to figure out we're somewhere in the Pine Barrens, which narrows it down to shit. The Pines stretch across more than seven counties in New Jersey.

Losing hope isn't an option, but I'd be lying if I said I wasn't.

Chapter Twenty-Eight
Danny
2003

Earlier that night

"It's fucking cold, man," Carson says, shivering in the back seat.

"Quit your bitching," I throw back. I woke up this morning with a phone call from Moretti. He gave us all some Nextel Chirp cell phones a while back, which are basically walkie-talkies that allow users to make phone calls, too, but they're only for him to summon us. He's still a firm believer in no business talk over the phone. He thinks everyone's listening.

Who the fuck knows.

"They'll all be together," Moretti said. *"Now's our opportunity to get rid of the opposition."*

He told us that Warren and his boys were having a big Christmas bash, so now was our chance to end our main threat. Warren has always been low-key doing shit, but the fact he's underselling us with shitty ass dope? It's fucking with Moretti's money, and it's killing our buyers because they're giving themselves more, thinking our dope is as cut as Warren's, and it's not.

Genesis

When Warren can't get his supply out fast enough, they're coming back to us. We've had more overdoses on our hands this past month than ever before, which is scaring our customers. Warren is screwing everything up. The stupid news thinks there's a bad batch, but that's not the case at all. It's fucking sad that's even news around here.

Mickey sits across the street with stupid ass Nugget and a few other boys, while Johnny, Carson, and I sit in Johnny's car outside of the bar Warren reserved just for him and his crew. Family day is over, and now the men party with enough heroin and hookers to keep them busy all night. They have no idea it's all about to be over. We've been sitting here for over an hour now, but there's only a handful of them. Warren doesn't have a big crowd of men working for him yet, but that'll change if we don't stop it.

Mickey will take care of Warren, and the rest of us will handle the leftovers. Carson takes a swig of the moonshine in the back.

"Don't get drunk," I tell him. "You need a clear mind."

"Don't fucking worry about me," he says. "I gotta make sure I don't freeze to death, or I won't be pulling a trigger on anyone."

Johnny looks over at me. "Nice having you around some," he says.

"Oh, you gonna get all sappy on me now?" I ask.

"You miss me, mother fucker?"

He scoffs. "Fuck you."

I hit his arm before rubbing my forehead. I need a cigarette.

We had a moonshine run after the meeting this morning, which meant driving nearly two hours to Robin County. All the liquor stores are closed due to Christmas, which means money for Moretti. We've doubled the price. Even the cops have bought some. Moretti's drug dealers have been selling like crazy. Christmas Day is busy. It's a moneymaking day for everyone.

I'm glad I spent yesterday evening with Bexley. Between tossing out moonshine, refilling the drug dealers' supply, and dealing with the cops who want to actually be cops, I haven't had a chance to catch my breath. Ma will be disappointed I haven't come by. I didn't even get to see Paul. I hope he spends the night before he goes back to school.

I need to at least call Bexley and tell her Merry Christmas. I wonder what she's doing. How her day went. Fuck, Carson's right. It is cold as shit.

"Get ready," I hear from my phone. "They should be good and shit-faced by now."

"You heard him," I say to Johnny and Carson. I press the side button on the phone. "Ready when you are."

I look over at Johnny as Mickey and his crew climb out of the car.

Genesis

"Never get caught," he says.

"Never get caught." He offers his hand for me to shake as Carson climbs out.

We dip around the building, and I pull out my gun from the back of my jeans, holding it down as Mickey signals that he's going in through the back. That's when I hear the first pop, pop, pop. Women scream as they run out of the building. I run toward the back door, just as a big ass motherfucker comes charging at me, knocking me on my ass. The gunshot almost deafens me as it hits the man on top of me, and I feel the heaviness of his dead weight when he slouches. I look behind me, seeing Carson.

Chaos erupts and more gunshots are fired. I shove the dead guy off of me and stand, seeing Johnny fighting with one of Warren's men. Another guy comes up behind him, but he doesn't realize I'm watching. I run up, and he turns around just as my brass knuckles connect with his jaw. I feel his bone give, and blood splatters from his mouth. I hit him again, and again, moving my hair away from my forehead when he slumps down.

I look to my left, seeing Carson pull the trigger like he's at fucking target practice and hitting all his marks.

The room is smoky and low-lit. The smell of kine bud and cheap women filters through the air. In my peripheral, I see a chair lifted. I raise my arm, protecting my face as the wood smashes down on my forearm. I wince and charge at the man, slamming him backward on a table filled with beer and overfilled ashtrays. He reaches for his gun, but I beat him to it, shooting him in the face.

My eyes widen at my quickness and I hastily wipe at the guts painted on my face and then look at my bloodstained fingers.

"It's done," Mickey says, coming out of a room I didn't even notice. The rest of the men and women have exited the building and it's just Johnny, Carson, Nugget and their guys, and me. Breathing heavy, I look at Mickey, who out of nowhere starts smiling. "We fucking did it," he says.

Carson holds up his gun and shoots it in the air, and that's when I realize maybe I'm dark, maybe I love this a little more than I should, but I'm not as fucking crazy as some of these men.

"You almost shit your pants," Nugget says to me, laughing.

"What the fuck did you just say?" I ask, stepping toward him. "I just shot a man in the face and you're coming at me with that shit?"

Johnny holds his arm out, putting it against my chest as Nugget smiles, showing me his ugly fucking tooth.

"I should knock your fucking teeth out."

"Come on, little boy," he says, holding his hands up and moving his fingers.

Genesis

"Chill the fuck out, Nugget," Mickey says. "Moretti will slit your throat if you mess with Danny, and you know it."

"Yeah, 'cause Danny is his little bitch."

I shove Johnny's arm out of the way, charging at Nugget. His smile widens when I grab his collar, pushing him against the wall as I put my gun to the side of his temple, digging into his skull with my finger on the trigger.

"Go ahead," he says, lifting his chin.

"Danny," Johnny says from behind me. "You can't do that, man."

"Let him go," Mickey says.

I bare my teeth at this smiling piece of shit. "One day," I say with a smile of my own. I grow closer to his ear. "You're going to be alone. You'll have no one to save you, and that's when I'll come, for I am the devil in human flesh. I'm in your nightmares, in everything bad that you do. The underworld is without a prince because I am here." I quick-kiss him on the cheek and push off. He wipes at his face, looking disgusted and honestly a little scared. I smile, my eyes as dark as the walls of hell. I don't know...maybe *I am* just as crazy.

"Who's gonna clean this shit up?" Slim, one of Mickey's men, says.

Johnny speaks up. "We'll burn it all."

"There are too many witnesses," Nugget says, still looking at me.

"No one's saying shit," Mickey tells him as Johnny lights a smoke. Slim grabs a bottle of whiskey, taking a sip before he starts dumping it.

"Half the girls are fucked up and they're too worried about making money to rat on anyone. We're their customers."

I nod in agreement. "We need to get the hell out of here."

Johnny sets the fire and we all run out as smoke starts filling up the place.

"We need to lay low," I tell them, climbing back into Johnny's car. "Head to Ma's. Paul should be there. He'll say we've been there all night if any cops want to ask any questions."

Samuel is the only one I worry about, but I don't say this out loud. Hell, even Ma will vouch for us, but Samuel is a wild card.

We hurry to Ma's, and once there, we jump out and run inside. I don't look toward the living room before I run up to the bathroom to clean up. I turn the shower on, looking at my reflection in the mirror above the sink. Blood is on my face, and I splash water on it, watching the crimson river flow down my skin and drip from my chin. The look on that man's face when the bullet went through it... The feeling of taking another man's life still tingles my fingers. Grabbing the bar of soap, I scrub the blood off before removing my clothes and stepping into the shower.

Genesis

After wrapping a towel around my waist, I run a comb through my hair, looking at my chest and seeing a bruise start to appear from where that man charged me. My hands are sore from hitting the other guys, but we're alive, and I hope we don't have to deal with any of this shit for a while.

Moretti's got half the police force paid off, but there are a few who will look farther into this. I just hope we didn't leave any evidence behind, and I hope Mickey is right about the girls keeping quiet.

I grab my cell from the counter and open the bathroom door, finding Paul standing on the other side. His eyes bounce down to my chest.

"Merry Christmas, bro," I say, moving past him so I can get dressed.

He nods, following me into my bedroom. "You've been busy all day, huh?" he asks. I look back at him.

"Yeah, been a busy fucking day. I open my drawer and pull out some boxers and a fresh pair of jeans. "Hey," I say, turning away from him and dropping my towel. I slide the boxers on before stepping into my black jeans. "I need you to do me a favor."

"What's that?" he asks.

"If the cops happen to come by, I need you to tell them we've been here all evening."

He crosses his arms, narrowing his eyes. "And where have you really been?"

"You don't need to know all that. Just vouch for us, okay?"

"Yeah," he says. "No problem."

"Will you talk to Samuel, too? He'll do it for you."

"I'll take care of it."

"Thanks," I say, taking a seat on the bed as I grab a smoke from my nightstand.

"You know Ma doesn't like you to do that in the house."

"Yeah, but it's fucking freezing out." I rest my elbows on my knees as he walks over to the window and lets it up. Running my hands through my hair, I exhale the smoke after I light it, and he walks over and shuts the bedroom door.

"How's everything at school?" I ask him.

"It's fine." He takes a seat beside me on the bed.

He's silent for a moment, and so am I, replaying tonight's events.

That guy's face when I shot him. Jesus Christ. How that shit doesn't affect a person just a little, I don't know. It needed to be done, though. It was him or me, simple as that. I take a drag from my smoke, looking down at the floor as the cold breeze comes in through the window behind me. Shit, this isn't worth the cigarette. I stand with my jeans still undone, hitting the smoke hard one more time before I toss the thing out the window and slam it down.

Genesis

"I always knew you were getting into some bad shit," Paul says. "I saw it in you when Dad was alive. You were always near him, always listening to the shit he had to say about life. All his genius Irish philosophies. And then, one day Johnny's dad just burned up in his house, and you two changed."

I watch the back of Paul's head as he speaks, wondering where he's going with this. Wondering what all he *really* knows. I had the idea he was too busy with his studies to pay attention to Johnny and me, but I'm thinking I was wrong.

"I know you had something to do with that," he says, looking back at me. It was done nicely, though. You two really made it look like an accident. Like the man just drank himself to sleep with a lit smoke and boom, just like that, he was gone. So conveniently for Johnny," he adds.

"What's your point here, brother?" I ask, walking over and leaning back against my dresser.

He shakes his head. "My point is, I want better for you, but I know it's who you are. It's in your blood."

"Is it not in yours? You're going into fucking politics. That's the devil's playground."

He chuckles. "You're not wrong."

I cross my ankles, sliding my hands into my pockets.

Paul looks at my chest. "That's some bruise you got there."

I shrug. "It'll fade."

He nods, rubbing a hand over his watch. "Samuel is not like us, brother. He's too good. He'll have a good life, an easy life. But you and me, we chose paths that'll kill us both. Me," he lifts a shoulder, his lip dipping at the side, "probably with a heart attack and you from a bullet. The less he knows about this shit, the better. I'll talk to him, but this will be the last time. You need to move out. You need to stay away from here as much as you can."

"Okay," I agree.

"As for Bexley," he says, standing up, crossing his arms over his chest.

My heart thumps an extra beat; my eyes tighten.

"She called earlier. I'm not sure where she was, but I know she wasn't at home, and she doesn't have a cell phone, right?"

"No."

He nods. "She was upset, Danny. Like really hurt."

She was upset. *Why?*

"You know in the end, you're going to crush her. Why don't you stop it now before you get in too deep?"

I smirk sadly. "I think it's too late for that, Paul."

He sighs. "You love her?"

"You know I do."

"Nah, we all love her. I mean, do you *love* her?"

Genesis

"Yeah."

"Then let her go. Let her have a good life, like she deserves."

I look to the floor, running my eyes over the carpet. "Just like Dad let Mom go?" I ask.

He scoffs. "And look where that got both of them."

I slide my hand from my pocket, running it over my chest, grabbing the knot on my necklace and running it between my thumb and finger. "You think they would have changed it knowing how the end would be?"

He shakes his head. "Probably not, but it's not too late for you two. She's young. You're both young. She'll find a good guy who'll make her happy."

I lift my chin, looking my brother in the eye as my heart splits. "And that's what I'm afraid of."

His eyes grow sad, and he walks over, gripping my shoulder with his hand. "Life's about making tough choices even if they hurt."

I know he's right. Goddamn, I know he's right, but that doesn't mean I'm going to listen. How am I supposed to let Bexley go? How am I supposed to watch her be happy with someone else? Just the thought alone causes me to see red.

"I'm gonna go talk to Samuel." He pulls me in for a hug. "Take care of yourself, Danny. I'll be leaving in the morning. I probably won't be back for some time."

I wrap an arm around his back and give him a squeeze. "You, too," I say. "Love you, brother."

As soon as he shuts the door behind him, I grab my cell phone and call her house. Her uncle answers.

"Hey, can I talk to Bexley?" I ask.

"She's not here. She called and said she was spending the night at a friend's house earlier."

"Oh," I say, my mind racing. *A friend's house.*

"Why didn't you come by today?" he asks.

I drop my head back, remembering on a whim I told her I'd stop by for Christmas. *Oh fuck.* I run a hand from my forehead to my chin, feeling a tightness stretch across my back.

I clear my throat. "Busy day. Family stuff. Umm, just tell her I called, would ya?"

"All right," he says. "Hey, Danny?"

"Yeah?"

"Don't hurt my niece, okay? She's had enough of that for a lifetime."

A ball of fire sits between my lungs, burning with guilt, shame, and lies. Because even I know she'll be hurt by the end of all this. We both will.

"I don't plan on it." We hang up and I walk over and grab a long-sleeve shirt and a clean black hoodie before putting my phone into my pocket. I grab my keys and walk into the bathroom to get my

Genesis

wallet. Running downstairs, I look to the living room, seeing Johnny and Carson watching *National Lampoon's Christmas Vacation*. Both have a beer. The light is on in the dining room, so I walk past them to say hello to Ma.

"Merry Christmas," I say to her. She looks up from a puzzle she's working on.

"Danny, where on God's earth have you been all day? Bexley has been calling up a storm."

"Sorry, Ma. I had to work."

"On Christmas Day?" she asks.

"Yeah, some people do." I reach down and give her a hug and kiss her cheek as I look at the puzzle. I check out the picture before grabbing a piece and sliding it into place.

"Wanna sit down and help me work on it for a while?" she asks.

"I gotta go talk to Bexley, but some other time, okay?"

"Yeah, you go and talk to that sweet girl. I'll see you later."

"Love you Ma."

I head out of the dining room, walking past the boys. "Y'all can stay in my room if you'd like. I'll be gone for the night."

"Where are you going?" Johnny asks.

"Gotta fix things with Bexley. I fucking forgot I told her I'd stop by her uncle's for Christmas."

"She'll be good and pissed," Johnny throws back.

"It'll make for some good sex," Carson says.

I kick his leg. "Shut the fuck up."

"I'll talk to y'all tomorrow. Give me a ring if anything comes up."

"Will do," Johnny says.

Chapter Twenty-Nine
Danny
2003

Ships from the river moan in the not so far distance as I jump into my Monte Carlo. Bexley is not at a friend's house. She's at the lake house. Putting my foot on the clutch, I start the car and pull away from the curb. I pop my thumb knuckle as I drive away from the neighborhood, looking to my left when I see Officer Radcliff sitting in his car eating a fucking donut.

He doesn't know I got a new ride, so he has no idea it's me, thankfully. I know he'd pull me over and ask a thousand questions about the bar we set fire to only an hour ago. I shift into third gear when I make it to the highway, hurrying so I can get closer to the girl I love.

I don't give a shit what everyone says. We're meant to be together, and now I feel like I've got to reassure her because I fucked up again. The thought of her waiting for me all day has me grabbing my smokes and twisting my hand on the wheel.

Minutes later, I'm pulling down the moonlit driveway, and that's when her car comes into view. I exhale relief.

She *is* here.

Paige P. Horne

Parking the car, I yank the emergency brake up and hop out, tossing my smoke. I hit the front porch steps, walking right in because the door isn't locked. I never gave her a key, but she's seen me grab one from under the dead plant.

"Bex?" I call out, walking from the living room to the back of the house. The bed is empty.

"Bexley?" I say again, checking the bathroom.

My pulse accelerates, pounding against my rib cage. Where is she? Panic starts to creep in as all kinds of bad shit goes through my mind. Has someone found out this is where I live? Did Warren have boys we didn't take care of and they've already retaliated?

But as I walk back through the living room, I spot the reason my heart beats. In a black coat and a beanie on her head, she stands on the dock down by the lake with the camera I bought her. Sliding the deck door open that's unlocked already from her slipping out, I step onto the porch. Snow crunches beneath my boots after I descend the stairs. Hair that's still a little damp from my shower freezes my neck, causing me to slide my hoodie up.

She doesn't hear me yet, and I like that. I stop before I get too close, watching her snap pictures of the icy lake as it glows in the moonlight. It's a beautiful sight, and not just the landscape. In my mind, years pass. The sun soars across the sky

Genesis

quickly, the moon taking its place just as fast. Boats drive across the lake, and ice melts and reforms.

I envision a life we could have together. I picture her wearing a ring I picked out, and me calling her my wife. I know it's stupid and we're way too young for all of that, but when you know...I think you just know.

I walk closer, and as soon as I step onto the dock, it shifts a little and she turns around. Slowly, she slides the camera into her pocket, and her hands follow as she walks toward me. Once she's close enough where I can see her face, my heart dives.

She's puffy-eyed and frowning.

I've hurt her...*again*.

"I'm sorry," I say on a rush. "The day slipped past me. I fucking forgot."

Glossy eyes have never looked more disappointed. "You said you'd come by. I waited."

"I know. I'm sorry."

"How many times will I hear that?" she asks dissonantly.

I swallow, panic creeping up my throat. I run a hand over my mouth. "I don't know." And it's the most honest answer I can give her, but it's not what she wanted to hear.

Disheartened and dissatisfied, she looks toward the lake. "I don't know what to do here, Danny."

"Let's go inside. We can talk about it."

Her eyes focus back on me. "Talk about it? Can you really tell me what you've been doing all day?" She smiles, but it's not from bliss. "Do I even want to know?" Her hand goes to her mouth, covering her lips, and she shakes her head. Tears fall, and like the water behind her, my heart freezes.

I don't respond because she already knows the truth. And part of me already knows she's backing out.

But I fight.

"I love you, baby. I'll do better. I promise I won't keep you waiting again."

"How can you be so sure?" she asks, and there it is. A small, oh so tiny, bit of hope. It's in her voice. It's on her face. I grab onto it like I'm hanging off the edge of a building and it's the only thing keeping me from hitting the pavement.

"Because I know. I'll make sure of it. I'll plan in advance, and I won't tell you I can be there if I know I can't. You won't be disappointed in me again."

She sniffs and rubs her red-from-the-cold nose. Her eyes go to the heavens. Exhaling, she murmurs, "I'm so stupid."

"You're not stupid."

Wiping at her face, she looks back at me. "I wish I didn't love you. This would be a lot easier."

"But you do," I say, my eyes not looking away from hers.

Genesis

I smile, hoping she's giving in. She respires again, rolling her eyes at me, clearly still mad, still upset, still hurt. She shudders. "I'm freezing. Let's go inside."

"Okay," I say as she starts to walk. I bite my inner cheek, wondering how this is going to go. Wondering if she's really going to forgive me. I need her to.

God, I need her to.

Once we reach the door, she slides it open. The heat thaws my skin, and I shut out the cold quickly.

She removes her coat, tossing it onto the chair. Standing before me in a beanie that makes her look adorable and a hunter green sweater, she narrows her eyes. "You've got one more chance, Danny. You fuck up again, and that's it for us. I can't keep doing this. I know you are who you are, and God knows I don't like what you do, but I...I love you and I hate myself for it. I hate what I'm becoming."

Tears form in her eyes, and she has no idea how much I hate myself for all of this.

"I'm sorry, love," I say. Reaching out, I pull her to me. She grips my hoodie. "I won't hurt you again. I promise."

I kiss her hair, inhaling her shampoo. "I love you so goddamn much."

Trusting me with her heart, she unhooks her fingers from the black cotton and wraps her arms around my back. We stand like this for a beat, and then she says in a heartbreaking tone, "Don't make a fool out of me."

I build us a fire and we pop in a movie. Bexley has still got her guard up, and I know it's going to take some time to let it down, but she's spending the night. One of the things I got her for Christmas was a strapless nightdress, and she's got it on. We sit on the couch, her on the other side, far away from me. It's odd. We're usually all over each other. But she's hurt.

"Come over here," I tell her.

She looks at me. Her hair is pulled to one side of her shoulder, revealing her slender neck. A neck I want to taste. Her nipples show through the cotton fabric. Camellia knew what she was doing when she picked this shit out, and I think Bexley knows what she's doing, too. She could have just worn one of my shirts, which might have turned me on more.

"I'm fine right here," she says, looking back at the movie, acting disinterested in me.

I lift a brow, my tongue darting out to my bottom lip as I watch her stubborn ass. She's spending the night. She's crazy if she thinks we're not going to fuck. Pissed, hurt, I don't give a shit. She's made a choice to work it out, so we're going to work it out.

Genesis

My eyes go back to the TV, and I run a hand over the side of my face. I need to shave. I stand up and walk over to grab my smokes, feeling her eyes on me as I go to the sliding glass door and open it a tad. Freezing wind swirls in. I light my smoke, putting my hand in my gray jogging pants and then looking back at her after I exhale. The room is too small for the chemistry we have. She can fight it all she wants, but I know she feels it, too. I catch her eyes on me, and I smile on the inside.

Look all you want, girl. I'm yours.

Bexley

Goddamn me and my hormones. Why does he have to look like that? I'm mad at him. I want to stay mad at him, but he's a walking sex show. In gray sweats that hang off his hips in the perfect way and a black T-shirt that does something to his dark eyes.

I'm trying so hard to fight this, but I'm spending the night for the first time. I'll be with him all night, and it's only eleven o'clock. Does he know how good he looks? His eyes go to me as I sit on the couch trying to ignore him, and I see a small smirk on his lips.

Yep, he knows.

Paige P. Horne

His smoke goes to his mouth, and he exhales out the door, giving me a moment to look at his neck, his Adam's apple. His arm flexes from in his pocket, and I look back at the TV before he can catch me.

Ugh, I'm very frustrated. I forgive him so easily and I make myself sick. Paul and Samuel must think I'm an idiot. He's turned me into a liar. My uncle thinks I'm spending the night with a friend, which I never do, but he's so wrapped up in Trinity, he probably isn't thinking clearly. I know they need alone time, too, so I'm sure they're glad I'm gone for the night.

I need some water. I stand up and walk to the kitchen. Grabbing a bottle from the fridge, I twist the top open and cool my dry throat. I hear the door slide back shut, and he walks to the back.

Thank God. It gives me a moment to get my shit together. I look to the floor. I know I said I'd give him one more chance and I am, but I'm so scared he's going to mess up again, giving me no choice but to end this. I can't be that girl who keeps forgiving. I won't be someone people feel sorry for.

I will end this if I have to. It'll kill me, but I will do it. He can't fuck up again. He just can't. I take another sip of my drink as he walks back in. He walks toward me, and I step out of the way so he can get to the fridge. Oh my God, he smells good.

Genesis

He must have gone and sprayed cologne on so he wouldn't smell like smoke.

I lean back against the counter as he closes the door. I watch as he drinks from the bottle, wiping his mouth with the back of his hand after. He gets these wrinkles on his forehead for no apparent reason. I feel like he has the world on his shoulders, and he's only eighteen. I have no idea what his life is like—only what he tells me, and it's not much. Not like when we were younger.

But that's for the best, I'm sure.

I can only imagine what he's done. The things he's done. Danny is a bad boy through and through, and it's not just show, and I'm messed up because it turns me on. But it's all fun and games until it starts to affect my life. I'm afraid one day it will. I'm afraid of a lot of things when it comes to this boy.

Mostly, I'm terrified he's going to drag me through hell and I won't put up a fight. Love is strange, it's unyielding, and causes you to make stupid choices. As long as the other person is with you, it doesn't matter that you're burning, because being without them is worse. And it's borderline pathetic how tough a game I talk when he's not right in front of me.

I will end this.

Yeah, right.

I'm done pretending I don't want him. We're in his house for a whole night, and we're not going to have sex? That's ridiculous. I put down my bottle as he watches me. Chemistry was made for us, and lust was built on everything we are together.

Danny is and always has been the guy I want. I knew the day I caught him running from a burning house. He was the cutest thing I'd ever laid eyes on. He had this look on his face that spoke volumes about who he was. He wasn't scared that he'd get caught. He was one hundred percent sure he wouldn't.

And even then I knew I had to know this boy. Danny is fire, mesmerizing and beautiful in all its colors, but he's dangerous, for he can destroy everything you are in a matter of moments. He's the fallen angel everyone is afraid of, yet how much fun is it when you listen to the man who rules the underworld?

No one ever broke the rules and said to themselves, *I didn't even have a good time.* Eyes like the darkness he loves watch me curiously. They dip down my cotton nightgown that I slid on just so I could see that expression. I grow wet from that look alone.

His hair is a ruffled mess from running his hand through it, and I wonder what he's thinking with a frown like that.

"Are we going to make up? Or are you just going to keep staring at me?" he asks.

Genesis

"You just can't stand me being mad at you, can you, baby?" I say in a mocking tone.

He lifts a brow in surprise. I'm sure he wasn't expecting me to say that.

"How about you stop doing stupid shit for me to be mad at?"

"How about I fuck you instead?" he says, and in one stride he's in front of me, grabbing my hips and kissing me with fresh minty lips. He brushed his teeth, too. His smell takes over my senses. His hands feel like the devil's touch and I want our clothes off.

Need swims through my veins like blood. My hands shake; my fingertips tingle. He reaches for the backs of my thighs, setting me on the countertop and spreading my legs with his body. The gown slips up to my upper thigh and he grips my skin like I'm going to run.

Like I'd ever.

"I went slow the first two times," he says, breaking our kiss as his open mouth finds my jaw and he licks the scar he caused there. "That's not going to happen now."

My hands go to his thick locks, and I tug so he'll kiss me again. His tongue moves with mine so easily it's as if we were made to kiss only each other. He reaches up, wrapping his hand around my throat, his thumb rubbing over my out of control pulse. Where has this guy been?

My head hits the cabinet behind me, but it doesn't hurt. Danny lets go of everything that is me and steps back. His eyes are blacker, his expression beautifully dark. "Take that off," he says, lifting his chin. My eyes bounce down to where he's most hard and my sex throbs.

Jesus Christ, will it always be like this between us?

I do as he demands and lift up, shimmying the gown over my head before dropping it to the floor.

In only black lace panties, my nipples pucker from his sight and the coolness in the air.

"And those," he says.

I lick my bottom lip, nerves tingling my spine. There's too much light in here, and I'm new at all of this.

"Don't be shy, Bexley. Do it."

I hate that he caught my hesitation. I wanted to seem braver than I actually am. But insecurities are a part of being human and he's been with women who get paid to do this. It sets a fire between my lungs. And I get mad for no reason. Anger gives me courage and I lift my ass from the countertop and slide my panties past my hips until gravity takes over and they slip over my legs. I wiggle them off my toes, letting them fall on top of the gown, and look at him almost in challenge. Maybe I am braver than I feel.

Genesis

I'm naked. Fully exposed and I could die if I wasn't so turned on by this boy.

"Spread those beautiful thighs, love."

God, I love when he calls me that. There's something so sexy about this bad boy using that term of endearment for me and only for me. I swallow, sliding one thigh over before doing it to the other. My ass is pushed out and I place my hands on my knees.

The look on his face could burn a whole forest.

"Slide your finger over your clit."

Fucking hell.

"You do it," I say.

He bites his grin. "No."

I try not to exhale, but I'm dying here. I feel almost dirty and I almost don't hate it. Danny's hand reaches into his gray sweats and I see his happy trial.

"Take your shirt off," I say. He shrugs, taking his hand out of his pants and lifting the back of his collar up and over his head. His back slouches, and his stomach muscles tighten as the shirt slips over his arms. He drops it beside my clothes and stands up straight, so confident. So boy, yet changing every day. My eyes go to his chest and the small bit of hair where his necklace sits. The necklace that matches my bracelet.

His hand goes back into his pants and he touches himself.

"Danny." I pout because I'm tired of playing this game. I want him. I need him to put me out of my misery. This is a lot.

He smirks. "What?"

"Come here," I say, reaching for him.

I see his chest fall and he gives in. He walks closer to me. "Don't ever be shy about your body around me, Bexley. This is you and me. Everything you do turns me on. Know that. Let that give you confidence. Now, touch yourself, and think about me doing it. How do you make yourself come when you're alone?"

He's close enough to kiss, but we don't. My forehead goes to his, and I think about all the times I've come with him on my mind. I may have moved away, but I never stopped daydreaming about him. And now here he is. In my personal space, so near I could lick his lips. I move my hand from my thigh and slide it over my clit. Moving it down to gather my slickness, I apply pressure and make circular motions, feeling the hardness of my most pleasurable place.

I gasp lowly, touching Danny's lips with mine. My eyes narrow, and I focus on myself until my thigh jerks. Dark eyelashes fan out over his cheeks as he looks down, watching me, and it's easier with him close. Our noses rub together, and our open mouths feather tenderly. He holds on to the countertop with white knuckles, and I grasp his

Genesis

forearm, feeling his muscles flex and his pulse beat against my fingertips.

 I feel sweat pool at the backs of my thighs, and I rub harder, pressing down until my head falls back against the cabinet and my toes curl as the sensation stretches my calf muscles and the pure, oh so amazing bliss, rushes between my legs. Teeth, lips, and tongue touch my neck as my chest heaves and my life source swims in crazy beats.

 "Goddamn," Danny says, bringing me back to the now. He grips my thighs, pulling me to him, and in a swift quickness, he buries himself inside me. His lips pout, his eyes slant, and he looks at me with a deep wonder.

 A deep breath comes from my chest, and he holds tight to my waist as he thrusts quick and fast, causing my boobs to bounce and my hands to slide from behind me. I reach up and grab the cabinet as he bends down and sucks my nipple, causing a tingling sensation between my thighs. I moan in approval and he switches to the other breast.

 "You like that?" he asks.

 "Yes." I move my hand and grasp the back of his head as he sucks and licks, biting slightly with his teeth. He fucks me harder, driving himself into me, filling me completely. A rush of wetness slides out of me as a new amazing orgasm shakes my legs and I cry out.

"Jesus," I pant, not expecting that. He smiles and keeps going. I pull him to me and kiss him with fervor, and moments later, his body jerks as he comes with a strangled moan.

He pulls out, his breath coming out in a rush, his head down as mine rests against the cabinet.

Running a hand through his hair, he coughs, looking at me and lifting his lips. "God, that was good," he says. I bite my own grin, breathing just as hard. His eyes look down my body, and he shakes his head slightly. "You're beautiful, you know that?"

I blush slightly now that the heaviness from being turned on has subsided, but I toss back, "You are, too."

Because he is. He stands before me, shirtless, just fucked hair, in gray sweats with his dick still out. I could go again just looking at him. Maybe later. After all, we do have all night. "Shower?" he asks.

I nod, jumping down and grabbing my clothes from the floor. He slaps my ass and pulls me flush against him, bending down to whisper into my ear, "I love that my cum is still inside of you. It turns me on that I'm the only one who's ever been inside of you."

I swallow, chills racing down my arms as his hand runs over my hipbone and down to my clit. He

Genesis

rubs it before sticking his fingers inside of me, and I feel his hardness on my back.

I moan as my head falls against his chest. God, will we ever grow tired of one another? Will this fade?

"Could you go again?" he asks, his voice deep.

I nod.

"Good. Come on."

Chapter Thirty
Danny
2004

Snow thaws and flowers bloom after the new year is celebrated. Bexley's birthday falls late spring. She's seventeen now and I tossed her a cell phone when she was sitting on my couch, eating a bowl of Ramen noodles and watching *Pimp my Ride* on MTV.

"It's been time for you to have one of those," I say.

I honestly hate calling her house and talking to her uncle. It's clear the prick hates me. Not that he doesn't have good reason. He isn't a stupid man. He knows I'm no good, but I love his niece and I'd knuckle up with the fucker if he ever tried to keep her from me. She smiles and opens the box, taking the pink Razr phone out.

"Wow, fancy," she says, flipping the phone open. She looks over at me in thanks.

"I got me a new one, too," I say, pulling the dark gray Razr from my pocket. "No more landlines." I can't use the Nextel Chirp for personal phone calls, so I needed a phone where I could call her at any time, and vice versa.

Genesis

"What? You didn't want a pink one, too?" she teases. I roll my eyes, grabbing a smoke from the table and placing it between my lips.

Time presses forward and I keep my promise to Bexley. I don't make plans when I know I can't keep them. In fact, I hardly make plans. It's better that way, and I think my girl digs the spontaneous moments we have.

I can't keep my hands off her. Every chance we get, we fuck until she's shaking in my arms. I know everything she likes now, and she's grown confident riding me until I come balls deep inside of her.

She's so goddamn beautiful it hurts sometimes.

Paul graduated from college this fall with a bachelor's in politics, and Samuel has been working full-time now with a construction crew. Ma is still attending Mass every Sunday and playing bridge weekly with her friends. I didn't totally ignore my brother's advice, and I moved out after Christmas. I keep my home a secret, though. Only Bexley knows where I live. Johnny doesn't even know, and he gives me shit about it constantly.

"It's smart to keep some things secret, Johnny."

"I didn't think we kept secrets," he says one morning as we ride out of town, heading to Robin County for a moonshine run. Winter has rolled in again, and the windshield wipers are doing their best to keep the snow off. Since the takedown of

Paige P. Horne

Warren and his crew, we've been laying low. We all were brought in for questioning shortly after that went down. But the thing about the law is, when you have no evidence, you have no case, and the fact we've been chill has helped it all blow over.

"Yeah, well, it's not personal. You know I love you like a brother and I don't tell them either."

"You've told her, though," he tosses back.

I look over at him. "I'm going to marry her one day, Johnny. You know that, right?"

He darts his eyes over to me before looking back at the road. "Yeah, man. I know."

And that's the last time he said anything about it. Winter passes, and once again a new year falls. It's 2006 now, the ground thaws, the trees fill with green, and Bexley turns eighteen. She started taking photography classes last year, and she's grown so good at it. There are photos of us hung all over my house, and I even blew some of her landscapes up and had them framed.

So this birthday, I toss her a different box. The best Canon digital camera on the market. She cries and I get rewarded with an afternoon fuck.

It's been a month since Bexley turned eighteen. She'll graduate this year, and I've been thinking a lot about the future. Bexley has been looking at colleges, and some are not so close. I don't discourage her, even though every time I see

Genesis

information about schools out of the state, my heart freezes.

I stand outside of the dressing room as women walk by, looking at me like I have horns or something because I've got a few tattoos now. Some show an interest they can't hide; some look at me like I'm the Prince of Darkness ready to yank them into fiery pits of Hell. I smile at all of them. Fucking judgmental cunts.

And when my girl comes out in a white dress with black polka dots spread out on the bottom, they look from me to her and shake their head, like I've forced this girl to choose me.

I flick one of them off, and she gasps in shock.

"Danny," Bexley says. "Don't do that."

"Can we go already?" I ask. "You look beautiful. Get that one."

I've seen her try on at least fifteen of these things. I need a smoke and some fresh air.

"You really like it?" she asks, looking in the mirror.

She looked good in all of them—well, except for the one that seemed to cut off her circulation. The back is open with a string zigzagging across until it ties at the dip in her back. It's spaghetti strapped and the skirt isn't too puffy like some of the others she tried on.

"Yes," I say.

"You're not just saying that 'cause you're ready to go, are you?" she asks with a lifted brow.

"No, love. I really like it. I'm fucking starving, though," I say as sweetly as I can muster.

She smirks. "Fine. This is the winner. Now I need shoes."

I groan inwardly, hoping this doesn't take near as long.

After she tries on several pairs, she decided on some black ones with a thin strap going across her toes. She looks hot in them, and I wonder if I can fuck her later with them on.

"You need a tux," she says.

"I'll handle that. Let's go eat."

"Nope," she replies. "I want to see you in a suit and tie."

"You will," I say as my stomach grumbles.

She hears it. "Wow, you really are hungry."

I take the dress bag from her hand and let her hold the shoes. "I told you. Let's ride. I'll get the tux tomorrow." My girl asked me to go to prom with her. Do I really want to get dressed up and go to some shit show with a bunch of high schoolers? No. But she skipped junior prom, so she's been hell-bent on attending this one.

"Okay," she says. "Hunger wins this round."

After we climb into the car, we head to a restaurant. It's crazy sometimes to think that we've been going out for a little over two years. There

Genesis

have been some rough times where we don't see eye to eye, but fighting with her is almost as fun as making up. "I'm really glad you said yes to going," she says as we slide into a booth and start looking over the menus.

"Well, who else would you go with?"

She rolls her eyes. "I wouldn't be going, I guess."

I nod. "Damn right."

Her phone vibrates, and she takes it from her purse.

"Who's that?" I ask.

"I don't know. I haven't looked yet. Nosy." She flips open the Razr I bought her last year and reads the text message.

"Well?"

"Geez. It's none of your business who it is."

I narrow my eyes. "Actually, it is."

She closes the phone and puts it back into her bag.

"Actually, it's not."

"Are you trying to pick a fight?" I ask.

She narrows her eyes, lifting her menu just as the server walks up.

She asks us what we want, and we tell her before she walks off.

I sit back in the booth, looking at the girl who won't tell me who messaged her and trying to figure out why she doesn't feel the need to tell me. I bought her that fucking phone. I pay the bill on it. I'll cut the damn thing off if she wants to play this game, although she could pay her own bill. She started working at a flower shop on the north side of town last year. There's no need for her to work, but just like she's doing now, she fought me on it. I recall the argument.

"I'm seventeen, Danny. I need my own money."

"I can give you money if you need it."

She shook her head at me in annoyance. "I don't want your dirty money. If I want something, I want to be able to buy it myself."

"So some days, I'm just not going to be able to see you? I mean, you go to school until three and then you'll be at the flower shop until it closes."

"We'll see each other still. Don't be so dramatic."

It hurt that she was just shrugging this off. Did she not want to spend time with me? But I didn't want her to see how she'd turned me into a little needy bitch.

"Whatever, Bex. Do what you want. You will anyway."

I didn't win that argument, but I'm not dropping this one. We'll get through dinner first because I am starving.

We don't speak throughout the whole thing. I eat and she picks at her food.

"You done?" I ask.

Genesis

She nods.

I sigh, toss down some money for the bill, and stand. She looks up at me before standing and we head out to the car, me lighting a smoke along the way.

She opens her door and I start the car after I climb in, too. After rolling down the window, I look down at the wheel, trying to figure out what I'm going to say here. Why does she feel the need to keep this from me?

How often is she talking to other people? I shake my head slightly. I don't mean other people. I mean guys. She's with them all day at school. She's a fucking catch, too, so what's stopping them from trying to pursue her? Why wouldn't she pick someone her age who's got a better future planned out for himself? Not some street kid who does things that are on the wrong side of the law.

I hit my smoke as the engine idles, and then I press the clutch, shift into reverse, and back us out of the parking lot, heading to my house where her car is.

Chapter Thirty-One
Danny
2006

Moments later, we're pulling down the drive, and we both climb out.

"Are you going to tell me why you don't want me to know who you're talking to?" I ask.

She looks over at me as we walk into the house. "Because it's none of your business. I can talk to whomever I want."

I slam the door shut behind me. "I'm your boyfriend, Bexley. That means it is my business."

"So what? You think you own me or something because I'm your girlfriend and I have to tell you every little thing I do?"

I step closer to her. "Yes," I seethe.

She laughs coldly. "You're kidding me, right?" I go to grab her purse as anger explodes in my chest, but she moves it from my reach.

"Give me the phone, Bexley."

"No." She walks over and snatches her charger from the wall.

"I bought the fucking thing. I'll break it into a million pieces."

"You see, that's why I wanted my own job, so you couldn't throw that kind of shit in my face."

Genesis

"Like I've ever done that."

"You're doing it now. Break it for all I care. I'll buy my own," she says, all matter-of-factly.

"I'm doing it now because you're keeping something from me."

"Oh, like you don't keep things from me."

"You know that's different."

"How?" she asks, raising her voice.

"It just is, Bexley."

"Yeah, because you're probably murdering people."

My jaw tightens.

"You think I'm an idiot. I know you're not a good man, Danny. I know you do bad things. I see the blood on your clothes, your gun in the bedroom."

I ignore all of that, except for the fact she just said I wasn't a good man. I know the truth in those words, but the fact she thinks it…it burns my lungs. "Are you fucking somebody else?"

Her face turns crimson and she slaps me. I narrow my eyes, opening my jaw.

"If you were a man, I'd knock the fuck out of you."

"Yeah, well, if I were a man, I wouldn't be here. You can't even trust your own brothers to know where you live. Why is that, Danny? Why can't you tell anyone? Do you have that many enemies you're afraid they may come for you in the middle of the night?"

I pinch the bridge of my nose. "What the hell are you doing right now, huh? Why are you doing this?"

"I'm glad. At least I now know you think I'm a slut."

I blink at her. "Why else would you hide who you're talking to? You spread your legs so easily for me, why wouldn't you do it for someone else? One of those preppy pricks at your school."

She shoves me, slapping me in the head and chest. "Like you aren't fucking any of those whores at the clubhouse."

"What? I wouldn't do that." I grab her arms, stopping her from hitting me more.

"But I would?" she says, her voice cracking.

I shrug, letting her go. "Seems like you are."

"Fuck you, Danny." She walks toward the door, but I follow, slamming it closed when she goes to open it.

"Let me go."

I yank the purse from her arm and grab the phone. She reaches for it, but I shove her arm out of the way as I flip it open. I look at the messages from none other than...*Samuel.* Lots of them.

There're questions about college and prom and other shit that I'm not included in.

Genesis

My eyes jump back to her. I feel like my guts have been ripped out.

"What is this?" I ask. "You've been talking to my brother behind my back?"

"My friend," she says. "We've always been friends, Danny."

My jaw clenches, and I squeeze the phone, nearly cracking it, but then I stop myself. My heart splinters like broken glass. I shake my head, slapping the phone shut like a director's clapboard because here's the real show. Here's the truth. She's been talking to my brother. The good one of us O'Brien boys. The one who could give her the better life Paul was talking about.

"Would you rather have him?" I ask quietly.

"No," she says, her anger melting. She walks over to me, taking the phone and tossing it onto the couch. "I love you." Her hand goes to the side of my face and I relish in the feel of her touch. On tiptoes, she brushes her lips against mine. I'm hesitant at first as our noses graze. My eyes look into hers, and then I wrap my hand around her waist, gripping her clothes as my mouth opens. Air rushes from her lungs, giving me oxygen to breathe again because the thought of losing her to my brother is unbearable.

Passion and love find solace in her arms. I reach up, touching her jaw and throat as our tongues dance to an all familiar tune. Her hands go to my shirt, and she rips the buttons off before yanking it from my shoulders. Fingers that now have tattoos reach for her breasts, gripping them in my hand. She moans into my mouth and quickly undoes her pants before breaking our kiss and stepping out of them.

My belt is unbuckled, my button and zipper next, and I lift her up into my arms as she wraps her legs around me. We find the floor and I grip her hips, lifting her up for a moment so I can fill her.

Her head falls back as she moans and rocks. Heavy breathing comes from us both, and I swear I would die if she ever did this with another man.

Her hand goes to my throat and she squeezes, looking down at me as she continues moving slowly.

Goddamn.

"I love you," she says. "Don't ever accuse me of being a whore again. I only do this for you. This is only for you."

I groan in bliss. "Okay, love. I know, I'm sorry."

She places her hand on my lower stomach and cries out when I flex upward. I bend, coming face to face with her, snaking my hand up her back and gripping her shoulder. I fuck her, holding her neck with my hand. Her face turns and she brings my finger into her mouth as she comes hard. I follow, pounding into her with all the anger I felt earlier. I fall back and she moves off me. We lie side by side,

Genesis

panting, and then I look over at her just as she does me.

I smile and she grins.

And this is what love is.

I look up at the ceiling as my heart calms. "I'd like you to stop talking to my brother behind my back. I know you have a friendship, but he's in love with you, Bexley. He always has been, and it's not fair to either one of us for you to encourage him."

She doesn't say anything for a beat as the pulse hammers against her neck. "I'm not encouraging him. You can look at all the messages. I don't have anything to hide."

"Then why were you in the first place?" I ask disputably.

She sighs, looking away from me. "Because I knew how you'd react." Her eyes focus back on mine. "You'd think it was something it wasn't. I've been friends with Samuel since I was eleven. How am I supposed to stop that?" She exhales, her gaze focusing on the popcorn ceiling. "I don't want to hurt him," she murmurs.

"He's a big boy. He can handle it. He'll find his own girl." I get that she cares for him. Hell, I do, too, but this is fucked up. He shouldn't even be talking to her behind my back. It's wrong at best. At worst, it's disrespectful, and I won't tolerate it. I grab her hand, bringing it to my lips. "You're mine."

Paige P. Horne

She looks back at me. "And I'll hurt anyone who tries to take you from me. Blood or not. Don't put me in that situation."

She watches my lips as I kiss her fingers. "Do you understand?" I ask her gently.

She nods. "Okay. I understand."

Chapter Thirty-Two
Bexley
One month missing

Time slides by like a slug here. I've tried to yank open the door, grabbing it with my hands behind my back. I've screamed, I've kicked, and I've finally broken down and cried because I don't think we're getting out of here. The stranger comes by every two days now, feeding us crap and no longer leaving us with any water.

Danny hurts badly. He's stiff, and I can't imagine the pain his legs are in. Especially since he goes all day without getting up. The one thing about having nothing in your system is you don't have to use the bathroom, which is bad. We're dehydrated and extremely malnourished. Our skin has grown pale, almost translucent. Danny has a beard now, and his cheekbones are prominent.

I can feel my hipbones protruding more than ever against my forearms, and I know I look like death. Not being able to touch my hair and face. Not being able to look at myself, except through the reflection in the window, which is hardly a mirror.

I press my forehead against it, shutting my eyes.

"Why the flower shop?" Danny murmurs into the night. He's been drifting in and out of sleep lately. I'm worried sick about him.

I move from the window, walking over to him. "What?" I ask gently.

"The flower shop? Why did you stay? Why didn't you leave Postings?"

I shrug. "It's my home."

"But your photography," he says. "You were so good at it."

I nod. "Yeah, well, it was just a hobby."

"I never thought that. I thought you were amazing."

I smile sadly, wanting so badly to wrap my arms around him and hold him. My heart is breaking. My heart is already broken.

"Maybe I'll pick it back up," I say despondently.

Danny looks up at me, his eyes sickly. "Promise me."

"Promise what?"

"That when we get out of here, you'll go after it. That you'll leave this town and never look back."

For some reason, my broken heart shatters even more, and tears I don't have the strength to cry rush out.

"I promise, Danny. I promise." I get on my knees, placing myself between his. I rest my head on his chest. I feel his lips against my hair, and moments later, I hear his own tears.

Chapter Thirty-Three
Bexley
2006

I drop my phone onto the vanity as Uncle Hale knocks on the door. "Can I come in?" he asks.

I exhale nerves. "Yep."

The door opens and I stand, grabbing my lip gloss from the bed. "He's here," he says.

I smile, sad to say, part of me didn't think he'd show. Danny doesn't do plans. He promised me he'd never let me down again, and that was his way of keeping his word. I do like the spur-of-the-moment things we do, but he's gone against his own rules. He *has* set a plan, and he's kept it.

My heart smiles in relief because I would have been absolutely devastated if he didn't come. I feel my hands shake as I look at Hale. "Do I look okay?"

He nods. "You look great, kid." His eyes grow watery and I narrow mine.

"You're not getting all sentimental on me, are you? I'm not about to walk down the aisle or anything."

He rolls his eyes. "Thank God for that."

"Hey," I say, frowning.

"Kidding. Come on. We don't wanna keep the boy waiting."

"Right behind you." He nods, exiting the room. I look over in my mirror, making sure my makeup is good and my hair is all in place. I spray the curls one last time before giving myself a nod.

"Let's do this."

I walk out of the room, my dress shuffling as I make my way down the small hall, and then I turn the corner. Hale is ready with my camera like I asked him to be and Trinity is smiling. She helped me with my hair.

And then I see *him*.

He's handsome as hell in a black suit and matching tie. He looks roguish, with thick hair he tried to comb, but it's obvious his hands ran through it. He's nearly breath taking.

His eyes bounce down my body, and he grins ever so slightly in approval.

"All right, let's snap a picture," Hale says.

Danny hands me flowers instead of a corsage. That's Danny—always going by his own rules. I take them with a smile, and he pulls me close as Hale takes some pictures of us.

"That good?" Danny asks.

"Good," Hale says. I grab the digital camera Danny bought me instead of the Canon and slide it into my small purse so I can get some photos of us throughout the night.

Genesis

"Be good," Hale says. "Don't do anything…stupid," he tosses out. Trinity hits him with her elbow.

"We'll keep it PG," Danny says with a wink, earning a look from me.

"Be home before midnight," Hale says firmly.

"Okay," I say.

We exit the house and Danny stops, looking at me. "You look beautiful, love."

"You don't look so bad yourself."

He gives my lips a kiss and we head to the car, where he opens the door for me. I climb inside, making sure my dress doesn't get caught in the door before he shuts it.

The ride is filled with small talk and music, and once we get to prom, Danny is the perfect date. We slow dance and I introduce him to some friends, and then we see Samuel.

He walks over to us, and I feel the tension radiating off Danny.

"Hey," Samuel says. I smile at him. He looks so cute in a white tux with a red tie.

"You look beautiful," he says to me.

"Thank you."

"How about you fuck around somewhere else?" Danny says to him.

"Danny," I scold.

"You been talking to Bexley behind my back? Why don't you get your own girl, motherfucker?"

Samuel smirks. "You worried I'm going to take her from you? If you were such a great boyfriend, she wouldn't need to talk to me."

Before I have time to process what Samuel just said, Danny punches him in the jaw, but his jaw turns to mush, and Danny's hand gets stuck. Everyone's eyes widen and I try to help pull his fist out, but it won't budge. I pull harder until I fall back, hitting nothing, my arms flailing and my legs kicking as I plummet into a black abyss.

I jolt awake, blinking my eyes open from my bed. "Just a dream."

I sit up, running a hand through my hair before I reach over and grab my phone, checking the time. It's after ten on a Saturday. Prom day.

My phone rings in my hand, and I smile when I see it's Danny.

"Hello," I say.

"Hey, love."

"Hey," I reply with a smile. Danny sounds wide-awake, unlike me.

"You ready for tonight?"

"Yes." I pick at a string on my comforter, twisting it around my finger.

"I can't wait to see you in that dress. Better yet, take it off."

I feel a blush creep up my neck. "I can't wait to see you in a suit. You did get one, right?"

He chuckles. "Yeah, baby. I got one."

Genesis

I hear someone talk in the back. "Look, I gotta go. Busy day ahead. I'll see you at five-thirty. We'll go eat somewhere before."

A knock sounds on the door. "You up?" Hale says. "I got breakfast."

"Yeah, be out in a minute," I tell Hale. "Okay, sounds good. See you then," I say to Danny.

"Love you," Danny says.

"Love you."

Exhaling after I hang the phone up and shaking the dream from my mind, I toss the covers off, hanging my feet off the bed and looking down at my freshly painted toes.

I head to the bathroom, brush my teeth, and wash my face before throwing my hair up and heading out into the living room.

"Good morning," Hale says before he takes a sip of his coffee.

"Morning," I reply, going for the orange juice.

"You excited for tonight?" he asks.

I nod, filling my glass, thinking about Danny saying he can't wait to take my dress off, and then I scrunch my face because I'm thinking that in front of my uncle. Eww.

"Trinity said she'd help with your hair if you wanted her to?" he says. Trinity is a hairdresser and works at a little shop on Third Street.

"That would be nice. Tell her thank you."

Hale nods. "Cool."

I walk over to the bag of breakfast takeout. "McDonald's biscuits," I say, my stomach growling in approval.

"Fresh," he says, grabbing the coffee pot and refilling his cup. I remove my biscuit from the bag and grab some mustard from the fridge.

"Jelly?" I ask him.

"Some in the bag," he says. I shut the door and prepare my biscuit before heading into the living room to watch some TV. Hale joins me moments later, setting his coffee down and looking at his food.

"Something wrong?" I ask.

He sighs, clearing his throat and looking slightly uncomfortable. "So, this prom thing. What are your plans after?"

I shrug. "We don't really have any." I take a bite of my biscuit, wiping mustard from the side of my mouth with my finger before licking it off.

He nods, still staring at his food.

"You gonna eat it or look at it all morning?" I ask with a smirk.

He looks at me.

"Dude, what is up with you?"

He exhales again. "Look, I remember prom. I remember the parties and the drinking, and I remember what every guy in the place had on his mind for after."

Oh God.

Genesis

"Danny is older than you. But you're both grown now. Well, legally anyway. Don't let him pressure you into anything you're not ready for."

"We're talking about sex here, right?" I ask, grabbing a napkin he brought in.

"Obviously," he says with an eye roll.

I smirk. "Uncle Hale, that ship has sailed." He lifts a brow. "Come on. You're not stupid. Danny and I have been dating for like two years now. I'm eighteen, for heaven's sake."

"So?" he says. "Some people do this thing where they wait for marriage."

I toss the napkin onto the table. "Well, sorry to say, I'm not some people, and I'm sure you aren't either," I say with a lifted brow, knowing full well he and Trinity are sleeping together.

He looks back to the table like he was hoping for a different response.

"Are you disappointed?" I ask.

"You're careful, right? I mean, I know you're on birth control, but you're extra careful, right?"

"Yes," I lie.

"Good. Then no, I'm not disappointed. I just would hate for you to get pregnant by that…"

I narrow my eyes.

"Come on, Bexley. You know as well as I do what Danny looks like, and I've heard rumors about the boy."

"Danny loves me, Hale. And I love him. If anything like that were to happen, he wouldn't leave me alone with it."

"You can never be too sure about these things. I saw it several times growing up. It's all fun and games until life gets real, and then people bail."

"Look, let's not worry about that, okay? And please, don't listen to the rumors. Danny may have a certain look about him, but he's not a bad guy."

"He has *sinner* tattooed on his arm, Bexley."

I shrug. "Aren't we all?"

He shakes his head. "I just don't like the kid. I've tried, but you can do better."

This hurts me. In life, we want the people we love to accept the people we love, and when they don't, it puts a strain on both relationships. I know how Danny looks to the world, and at times, the stares from strangers really piss me off, but I try not to care because I know Danny doesn't. I know we love each other enough for it not to matter what everyone else thinks. But no matter how much you tell yourself that other people's opinion of you is their business, it still stings a little deeper than it should.

"That isn't for you to decide."

"No, it's not. But I think you're messing up here. I know you've been looking at schools away from here. I've seen the pamphlets. Don't let that guy stop you from living your life. If you want to go

Genesis

somewhere besides here, then you go. Live your life. Your mom would want nothing less."

I look over at him at the mention of Mom. "She liked Danny, you know?"

"She only saw the boy. She's not here to see what he's become."

"And what has he become?" I ask as anger fizzles my nerve endings.

"From what I hear around this town, he's a criminal. He's done some things."

"What things?"

"He's been seen beating up people. He's been seen riding around in that gangster car of his with guys who look just like him. There was a bar that caught on fire with some gang members in it a couple years back. I heard Danny was brought in for questioning on that, and you never said why he had to get a new car, so I can only assume it was his car that got shot up all those years ago."

I heard about the bar on the news, but Danny never mentioned the police had questioned him. I swallow, my eyes going to the coffee table as steam twists in the air from Hale's cup.

"You don't know about any of this, do you?"

My eyes bounce back to his. "Some things are better left unsaid."

His face turns crimson. "That's bullshit. See, I told you. He's a goddamn criminal, and here you are going to prom with him and acting like all of this is okay. You deserve better than this, Bexley."

Jesus Christ. Don't we all deserve better at some point with every relationship? People fuck up. We aren't a perfect race, and at times there's going to be one of you who gets it wrong.

So what?

You just walk away?

You just give up?

Who wins from that?

I shake my head, looking to the floor. Danny didn't just forget to call me or forget it was date night, though. Danny shows up with blood on his clothes and busted knuckles. I have this angel on one shoulder and the devil on the other, and I'm sick of it.

"Stop it," I say. "Please stop. You've said your piece. I don't want to talk about it anymore."

"I wish you would stop seeing him. I don't want you mixed up in all of that."

"Well, I'm not." I stand up, grabbing my food from the table. "If you won't accept my relationship with Danny, then I'll move out."

"What? And go where?"

"I'll figure it out, but I'm not going to listen to this every day."

He throws his hands up in surrender. "I'll drop it. I don't want you moving out."

Genesis

"Promise me you won't say anything else about it."

He runs a hand down his face. "Yeah, I promise. It's your life. You live it how you see fit." He gets up, too, walking over to grab his keys. "I'm going for a drive. I'll call Trinity about your hair. Eat your food. Have the house to yourself for a bit."

With that, he shuts the door behind him, and I release air I didn't even know I was holding.

I flop back down on the couch, and I can't control the tears that fall. I know Hale is right, and I hate everything about it.

Chapter Thirty-Four

Bones
One month two days missing

Bexley has slept against my leg the last three nights. Having her near helps, but I'm slipping. Even the strongest men fall eventually. I've been strong my whole goddamn life. I've fought, I've clawed my way to the top, and I've stayed there when I didn't necessarily want to.

During all that, I've stood by and watched the woman I love have a life with another man. I'm not sure what's been harder—being stuck here like a caged animal or witnessing another man get her smiles, her love, and her affection.

It's nearly killed me.

The sound of a truck pulling up has me lifting my head. I hear the door shut, but like always, the truck stays running, and moments later, I hear keys.

The stranger steps inside, holding two coats.

"Thought you two might like a little extra warmth."

I scoff, wondering why he's going through all the trouble when he plans to kill us anyway.

"Tell me," I say weakly. "How is your plan working out?" I want to laugh at this fool. I know Moretti is protecting my family, and this guy

Genesis

appears to be a one-man show. There's no way he could get through to them.

"Just fine," he says.

"Are you lying?" I ask skeptically.

"Come on, Bones. Do you really want to fuck with me?"

I tilt my head up, looking over his mask and the coats in his hand. "I must have really done something, huh?" I say lowly.

I see him tense up.

"I must have ruined your whole life for you to go to all this trouble." I shake my head. "Tell me, man who's so big and bad he has to hide behind a mask and voice disguiser. What was it? Did I fuck your wife? Did I kill your brother, your father? What did I do for you to keep us here like your little pets?"

He drops the coats onto the floor, going to the window.

I watch him.

"I've always thought you were a smart man, Bones. But it appears that you're not."

He gazes out, but I look down at Bexley. Her eyes are wide, telling me to shut up.

I smirk, but then I hear something that makes me turn stone-cold.

Snap, snap, snap. A rubber band cracking against skin. I look up at him as my mouth goes slack, my body starts to shake, and my chest caves.

No. Trig?

Chapter Thirty-Five
Danny
2006

"She's fucking crazy," Carson says from the back seat. "I fucked her once, and now I can't keep her away from me."

"Shouldn't have given her that golden dick of yours," Mickey says sarcastically from the passenger seat of my car.

He looks over at me and I smirk while holding on to the wheel.

"Hey, I'm serious, man. I think she's stalking me. Can't we ban her from the clubhouse or something?"

"We're not banning a chick from the clubhouse," Mickey says. "If you want her to leave you alone, then grow some balls and tell her."

I hit a bump and I hear Mason jars rattle in the trunk. It's well after lunch. Moretti got a new supply of heroin this morning, so we spent the better half bagging it. Now that Warren and his crew aren't an issue anymore, business has picked back up and the overdoses have stopped. We're headed back to the clubhouse with a fresh stock of moonshine and less heroin than we rode up here with because our guy asked for a little to try to sell.

Genesis

Meth is big around there, but he might be able to move some smack.

"Anyway," Mickey says to me, "Moretti has been in touch with a cocaine smuggler that lives in Atlanta who has a connection in Miami. I've already been down a few times to establish a relationship."

"What's his name?" I ask.

He looks over at me. "Simon. Motherfucker is crazy, Danny. This shit is going to take time, but there's money to be made, and you know Moretti's all about that shit."

I nod, looking back at the road. Moretti has these ideas all the time. He's always looking for more ways to make money.

Atlanta, though? That's far and a lot of traveling.

I decide not to worry about it right now. It's only in the beginning phase, and like Mickey just said, it's going to take time, probably even years before Moretti trusts the man enough to go all the way with this.

I squint from the sun and look in my rearview mirror. Traffic is busy per usual. I get over, grabbing my shades from the middle console, sliding them on, and noticing another car get over behind me when I dart my eyes back to the rearview.

I tilt my head, rotating my hand around the wheel as we head down the highway. Every so often, I glance up and notice the gray car still behind us. I turn my blinker on, slowing the car.

"What are you doing?" Mickey asks me.

"We've got a tail," I say. "This car has been following us since we parted ways with Rummy."

I turn down a two-lane road with the car still behind us.

"Pull down there," Mickey says. "Let's see why."

I turn off the paved road and stop the car. We four get out just as the guys in the other car stop.

"Are you following us for a reason?" Mickey calls out to them. I narrow my eyes, seeing Johnny holding his gun.

The driver gets out and the rest follow, walking toward us. Jesus Christ. They're fucked off meth.

"We want what you got in your trunk," the driver says, his jaw working.

"And what's that?" I ask.

"The moonshine and the drugs."

"Not sure what you're talking about," Mickey says. My eyes dart over to Carson who's got his hands behind his back, flicking the rubber band on his wrist right over the gun tucked in his jeans. Carson started going to therapy last year after he beat a guy in the clubhouse for taking his chair. He's got this thing now where he wears a rubber band when he feels slightly angered. It helps ground him…sometimes.

Genesis

"Shit," I say under my breath.

"I think you do," the passenger says.

"You need to go on back where you came from," I say. "There's nothing for you here but trouble."

The driver laughs, giving us a shit-eating grin. "We like trouble."

I sigh, and without a chance for any of us to react, Carson grabs his gun and shoots the driver. The man goes down, holding his throat as blood rushes out.

I swing and punch the passenger in the face, as Johnny takes on one of the boys in the back. The guy hits me in the jaw, clipping my lip, and I feel it when the skin breaks. Quickly, I grab my gun and knock him on the side of the head. He slumps down and a gunshot goes off.

"Oh fuck," Johnny says.

"Let's get out of here," one of the back seat guys shouts. "I didn't sign up for this shit." The two pussies run to the car, leaving the shot guy and the one I knocked out behind. I look over as they reverse out of here, dirt and gravel flying up, mixing with the severity of all this.

Mickey lies on the ground, holding his inner thigh.

I run over to him, dropping on my knees. "Fuck, man." My hands shake over his wound. I look back. "Get something from the car to wrap this up."

Carson runs to the car, and I hear gurgling from the guy who was shot in the throat.

He's dying, but he shouldn't have followed us. Goddammit, he shouldn't have followed us. Carson runs back with a towel and I grab it, placing it on Mickey's leg.

"Shit," he says, grinding his teeth.

"You're gonna be okay," I say. "Help me get him in the car." I point to Johnny. Johnny and I lift Mickey up and carry him to the car as Carson opens the door.

"What about those two?" Carson says, looking at the men on the ground. Mickey groans from the back seat, his face glazed with sweat. He wipes his brow with his bloody hand, causing a streak.

"Fuck them. We need to get him to a hospital," I say.

"Can't do that," Johnny says.

"Johnny, he's fucking bleeding out, man." Carson points out the obvious, but I know Johnny is right. They'll ask too many questions. Of course, we could lie, but they'll report it and we have a reputation.

"Either way, we need to drive," I say. No one disagrees and we climb into the car. Johnny hightails it out of here, and Mickey curses in the back.

"Take me to the clubhouse. Moretti knows a nurse. She can help."

Genesis

He lets out a strangled laugh. "I always knew this shit was going to get me killed."

"You're not going to die," I tell him, looking back. The towel is soaked with blood now. I'm no doctor, but this doesn't look good at all.

He's losing too much blood. His face is as white as a ghost. His eyes look to mine, and right then, I see fear and the truth. He is going to die.

"Go faster, Johnny. Carson, call Moretti. Get that nurse ready. Goddammit, what the fuck happened?" I say, slamming my fist into the dash. My hands shake as Mickey moans in pain. Johnny is going a hundred miles per hour, and Carson talks on the phone, using code to say our situation. I grab my smokes from the pocket door, lighting one as my mind races.

I look over at Johnny just as he looks at me. We say with our eyes what our mouths can't at this moment.

This is the life we signed up for. This is the shit show we chose. I look away from my friend, my eyes going to the window as thoughts chase each other.

What if I left this all behind? What if I took Bexley and got the hell out of here? I don't want to be Mickey, lying in the back seat, dying because of some stupid meth head.

"Danny," Carson says to me.

I look back as his eyes dart to Mickey. I twist, looking myself. My eyes shut for a brief moment and I take in a breath, making the sign of the cross over my chest.

"Slow the car," I say.

We head back to Moretti's in silence as the blackness of death surrounds us. I look at the dried blood on my hands and say a silent prayer for Mickey.

"What the fuck happened?" Moretti barks as we walk into the clubhouse.

Johnny takes a seat at the bar, and I lean back against the wall.

"Some fucking meth heads. That's what happened," Carson says, flicking his rubber band.

"Meth heads?" Moretti says. "You let some goddamn tweakers do this shit?" He looks at me.

"I didn't let anybody do anything," I reply lowly.

"Don't speak to me in that tone, Danny. This is a fucking shit show."

"I wasn't in charge. The man who was in charge is lying cold in Johnny's back seat!" I yell. I grab a bottle from the bar and throw it at the wall.

"Well, you clean it up!" he says. "Because you're in charge now."

Genesis

"What?" I ask unbelievingly. Nugget, who's sitting on the sofa, jumps up.

"He's in charge?"

"Yes. Get rid of Mickey's body and do it quickly."

I look over at Nugget, who narrows his eyes at me before he leaves the room. He should be in charge. He's been here longer.

"Let's go," Johnny says. "I know where we can bury him."

Moretti doesn't even want to see the man? He doesn't even shed a tear for the guy who pledged his life to him? My thoughts about Moretti change. My thoughts about everything change.

The moon is high in the sky now as Carson, Johnny, and I stand over Mickey's grave. We're deep into the Pine Barrens. Our hands are bloody, dirt-covered, and calloused as we each hold a shovel. We stand silent, worn out from the hole we just dug. The wind howls through the trees, sending a chill down my spine as animals scurry through the Pines.

"We better go before the Jersey Devil comes," I say.

Carson smirks. "You think he's real?"

Paige P. Horne

I shrug. "I don't know." I rub under my chin. "I don't know about anything anymore."

I feel Johnny glance over at me, but I don't return his look.

I sigh, looking down at the dirt Mickey's under.

"May the road rise to meet you. May the wind be always at your back. May the sunshine warm upon your face. May the rains fall upon your fields. And until we meet again, may God hold you in the hollow of His hand," I pray.

We three do the sign of the cross and head back, and as we climb into the car, a thought slams into my mind.

Prom.

Chapter Thirty-Six

Johnny "Sweep" Dolffi

I stand outside Bones' bar, hitting my smoke as the cold Jersey wind sweeps across my face. My boy has been gone for a month now. I've fucking searched everywhere. The cops have, too, only because Moretti is paying them otherwise. They don't give a fuck about Danny O'Brien, and it helps that Bexley's uncle has filed a missing person's report.

How can he just disappear? Both him and Bex? Did they plan this? Would he do this and not tell me? He's always had it bad for the girl. He'd mentioned getting out of this lifestyle when Mickey got popped, but I just can't see him not telling me.

We're boys. We're brothers. I've had this guy by my side since we were kids.

A few people walk into the bar. "'Sup, Sweep? Sorry about Bones, man."

I nod, hitting the joint between my fingers as I lean back against the wall, my eyes going to the concrete below me when I hear a truck pull up.

Trig gets out. "Why are you standing out here in the cold, man?" he asks.

"Too many fucking people in there," I say, passing him the joint.

He nods. "You and your introverted ass."

I shrug, looking at his boots. "Have you been playing in the mud?"

He looks down, too, blowing smoke. "Nah, went out to my dad's old hunting cabin."

"What the fuck for?" I ask, looking at his truck and seeing the tires are caked also.

"Needed some space."

"From what?"

"You sure are nosy all of a sudden," he says to me.

"Just never known you to need space."

"What, you're the only one who can be secluded?"

I shrug. "Whatever."

"Anything new come up about our boy?" he asks moments later.

"No. Still nothing."

I want to go into more detail about it with him, but honestly, Trig has been acting weird lately and disappearing for hours at a time. Now he comes here with mud on his tires and boots. I didn't even know his dad had a cabin.

Wait? I didn't even know about his dad.

"You said your dad?" I ask.

He nods, offering me back the joint, but I shake my head. "You've never talked about your family."

"Well, I am now."

Genesis

"Why were you in the foster home if you had a dad?"

"He's no longer here."

"So, he's dead?"

"That's correct," he says, dropping the joint and putting it out with his boot. "I'm heading in. I need a drink."

I nod, sniffing as he opens the door.

Three days later, I'm heading out of my house. It's early, and the sun has yet to blister the sky with orange and blue light. I stand by the car, breathing in, and then without thinking, I hop into my car and head to Trig's house.

It only takes me moments. He doesn't live far from where I stay. Placing my coffee in the cup holder, I grab a smoke and light it. Rolling the window down a bit, I hit my brakes when I see Trig walking out to his truck with what looks to be coats.

Pulling over, I place my cigarette between my lips and watch as he cranks the truck. His reverse lights come on, and he backs up, hitting the curb before taking off down the street.

And I don't know why—call it a gut feeling, one that has me feeling sick. One that makes me ask myself, *What am I doing? What am I thinking?*

Paige P. Horne

But regardless, I hit the gas and follow him.

To be continued…

Insurgent (Bones, Book Two) will be releasing soon! Add to your TBR on Goodreads:
Insurgent (Bones, Book Two)

If you haven't read the Give Me series yet, now's a good time. The first book is FREE!
Grab Give Me Love now!

Reviews mean so much to us authors. Please, if you enjoyed the book, make sure to leave a review.
Xoxo,
Paige P. Horne

Made in the USA
Columbia, SC
10 January 2025